POWER OF THE PIXIES

BOOK FIVE IN THE LEGENDS OF MYTHERIOS

JAMES KEITH

Power of the Pixies

Legends of Mytherios - Book Five

SYNOPSIS

War is coming…

Desperate to escape the grasp of the villianous dark lord, Dromos, Methira whisks Andy and Josie to safety. Only with her sisters by her side does she hold any hope of preventing Dromos' evil reign from descending on them.

Yet Lord Dromos' stronghold gets more powerful by the day. Leading an army of undead warriors, a familiar face stands at his side.

Will the united power of the pixies be enough to defeat his menacing army? Or will battling Dromos lead to their demise?

Power of the Pixies is the fifth instalment in the Legends of Mytherios series. Book six, Engulfed, is coming soon!

CONTENTS

PROLOGUE

THROUGH EONS, FAIRIES HAVE LIVED WITHIN the dense woodlands of Mytherios. They made their homes among the trees below, those on the hill overlooking the deep forests and within the rocks and gentle stream of the woodland. It was known all over Mytherios that when the sun slipped from the face of the sky, tumbling into the abyss of the west, the light from the fairies' wings illuminated the trees forming an array of beauty that could be seen by anyone within sight of the woodlands. There was never a light attending their flight, but their pure hearts radiated such beauty that everyone could see for miles around.

It was this quality that made them keepers of the peace in Mytherios. For centuries, they had been the mediators there, protecting their home and the rest of Mytherios. Led by their queen, Methira, they flitted through the woodlands ensuring that peace reigned on every side. They sat over cases of simple nature and over those of the most complex nature, and in all of these, they didn't abdicate their duties or shy away from difficulties.

Each day, just before the sun picked itself off the floor in the east, they would flit through the woodlands and elsewhere, making sure that everything was in the best order before the day commenced.

Everything was peaceful; all the wildlife of the vast forest thrived in harmony, multiplying as the days went by... until Dromos found his way into Mytherios.

Methira had felt the overwhelming stench of evil on the horizon the moment the monster landed in Mytherios, but there was nothing she could do. She and her ilk rested on the knowledge that the lord of the Underworld would not attack them if the fairies kept to their woodland home.

They watched his reign of terror begin. The murders, the maiming and the wickedness spread through all of Mytherios very quickly.

Then the evil day soon arrived. Dromos sent his evil spurn, Ratifi, and his horde of demons into the woodlands.

"Destroy them all, burn it all black," he instructed.

Ratifi bore fire in his hand as he matched right into their home, scorching everything with evil glee. The fairies died in their droves, but it wasn't just their lives that they lost; their home died before their eyes too. The beautiful flowering plants, the shrubs, the trees, and the beauty that overwhelmed anyone who looked upon it, were all destroyed. Everything was kissed by the tongue of Ratifi's flame, and soon all the beauty turned to lurid blackness. Everywhere became a vacant country. Ratifi sucked up the little stream that flowed through the woodlands and an ugly emptiness was all that was left of that once thriving home of the fairies.

But Methira, queen mother of all the fairies, had escaped with some of her fairy children, flitting away into the distant hills when Ratifi had appeared with his hordes. She had spirited as many fairies as she could out of the woodlands at the first sign of trouble, but she had also watched helplessly as many others were shot down by the fiery anger of Ratifi who reveled in his new task. He shot with reckless abandon, and many of the children of the trees and earth fell to his balls of fire.

Those who escaped with Methira went into hiding, keeping safe anywhere they could hide in the wide expanse of Mytherios. They became lonely, unable to sing when the darkness came, unable to light up the world as they had done in better times.

Methira would return afterwards to the woodlands, her gossamer wings flapping as she hovered over her former home. Tears filled her eyes at the sight of the burnt bodies of her people and the ruins of her own home. She mourned them with a shrill wail and an avalanche of tears, and then she went away into exile, never to be seen around there for many years.

CHAPTER ONE

JOSIE HADN'T HAD SO MUCH JOY ALL HER LIFE, at least not since Andy was spirited away by the Dark Goblin and she had been left to roam the world above and under in search of her brother. Now, her face was stretched from ear to ear with a smile and she couldn't seem to stop smiling. She stared into Andy's face, and every now and then, she found herself falling into his arms for a quick hug.

The two siblings were standing somewhere in the woodlands of Mytherios with Methira only moments after escaping the lair of the mighty Dromos, lord of the Underworld. Methira kept looking around the woodland with some pain in her eyes, a pain which Josie would have recognized, except for the fact that she was too deeply engrossed in her own happiness to notice Methira's sadness.

Suddenly, they heard a loud roar that shook the trees. It was strong and powerful, with the tops of the nearby trees feeling a short tremor.

"He is really angry," Methira said, staring off into the distance.

"He is a brute," Andy replied, staring off into the direction of Dromos' lair. He must be the one roaring so heavily, angry at the fact that Andy and Josie had escaped him with the help of the fairy queen. The loud roar had drawn Josie out of her reverie and for a moment, she realized they had so much yet to do if they were to defeat the demon that is Dromos. It was at this moment that she noticed the sadness in Methira's eyes. She recognized it; it was the sadness of one who has lost something valuable. She had worn that look through the difficult times she had lived without her brother by her side.

"There is a sadness around your eyes," Josie said to Methira.

"We all have sadness around our eyes," the fairy queen replied.

"Tell me about yours, who are you?" Josie asked gently.

Methira looked around the woodlands one more time, taking in the whole landscape, her eyes lighting momentarily on everything for a second.

"I am Methira, queen of the fairies who once lived in these woodlands in the years before Dromos came and turned our world to black soot. We had lived in harmony with all the other creatures who made their home in the woodlands. Dromos won't let us exist, even in this out-of-the-way home we have made for ourselves. He murdered my people, most of the fairies, burning them to death, turning them to charred dust."

She suddenly couldn't continue and paused her story, her eyes glued to something on the earth that reminded her of her people, of the life they once had and the abrupt end that it had all been put to.

"We couldn't even sing their final songs to pave their way to the world beyond this one. Their siblings had all gone into hiding for fear of being put to death, and I was the only one left above ground. One voice won't open the portal for their homegoing, my voice alone couldn't pave their way home, and so I weep continually for the lives lost, but my heart breaks each time I remember that they hover around us, unsung, unburied and undead."

Tears streamed down her face now and Josie held her, patting her gently, her own heart shredded by the pain she saw on the face of this gentle fairy.

"What of the ones that escaped? The ones that didn't die?" Andy asked.

"I have searched the length and breadth of Mytherios. I have walked this land and these sands, yet I haven't seen any of them. Not since that day, that evil day when fire rained upon our home. I shouldn't bore you both with my tale of woe. Come, I should take you to a place where you can get some rest."

So saying, she flitted above, lifting the two siblings with her as she flew up to a place high in the trees on the hill overlooking the woodlands. There was nothing to be seen except for the dense leaves of the trees bending into each other, but she flew past the dense cluster of leaves and placed their feet squarely on a plush surface. They were surprised to find themselves standing in an airy room. Josie looked around, savoring the beauty of the small home and enjoying the feeling of lush carpeting under her feet. Everything was white and glittering, and both Josie and Andy wondered at the same time how the fairies came to construct such beauty above the trees.

Josie hadn't seen anything as beautiful as this. Everything glittered and shimmered at the same time. She was lost for words. Andy sat in something that looked much like a plush couch, balancing his arms on the arms of the chair and winking at Josie. She smiled at him, turning her attention to Methira who was still roaming the whole place, touching one thing or another, pausing to look sadly over the things that were within the house. Josie walked up to her.

"I am thankful for all your help, Methira, but my brother and I have to head back home. I set out to find him and now that I have done that, everything is back as it should be, and we need to head back to our home."

Methira looked at Josie sadly. She had known the young girl's quest had been centered on her brother's rescue. She had fervently wanted to rescue her brother from the shackles that bound him, and no one could fault her, but there was a much bigger picture here. Both of them were part of something much greater than themselves, but she didn't know how to get them to help her. She sighed deeply. Without Andy and Josie, Mytherios could never be freed from the stranglehold of Dromos. The divine warriors were still trapped within Dromos' lair, and without them the world they had always known would never return to them.

"I think there is something you must know, Josie."

The younger girl watched Methira, giving her ear to the fairy as she began to speak to her of this thing that sounded so serious and grave that she had to listen attentively.

"Mytherios is under siege, held in the evil hands of Dromos, the lord of the Underworld, and his minions who have destroyed almost everything about this place which a lot of us call home. Even you have felt the impact of their wickedness on your world. Mytherios has to be saved from the hands of these monsters, and there is only one group who can save it: the Four Divine Warriors."

"Who are these Four Divine Warriors?" Josie asked.

"The Four are divine warriors that ruled over the affairs of Mytherios from time immemorial. They are rulers whose duty it is to administer justice and keep the wheel of our world running smoothly. But these men and women are being held hostage and are powerless in Dromos's lair."

"What do you want from us?" Josie asked, knowing the answer to her question even before the words had left her mouth.

Methira watched her, wondering how best to make her listen, to get her to help. These two children were the last hopes of her dying world. If they kept quiet, if they folded their arms and watched, this world as they knew it would fold into the palms of the dark lord and where would they be then?

"We need to free the Four Divine Warriors from the hands of Dromos, that is you, your brother and I. It is the last hope for our world. It is the only way Mytherios can be saved. Will you help me?" Methira asked. Her sky-blue eyes looked helpless, pleading in her depth as she sought Josie's help.

A terrified look came over Josie's face and she stared straight at Methira, turning her eyes now and then to her brother who seemed oblivious of the exchange going on between the other two. Her eyes were wild, and her pulse became slightly elevated. She calmed her thoughts, trying to bring herself down from the fear that had suddenly assailed her. She had frozen at the mention of heading back to Dromos' lair, it was the one place she wasn't willing to go to ever again.

It had taken all of her strength to go there for Andy; it had taken everything she had inside of her to tear through the fear. How would she say this to Methira? A part of her felt selfish. Methira had helped her to free her brother, and now that she needed her to come through for her, she was unable to do so.

"I am not strong enough to face Dromos," she began. "I cannot face him again. The last time I did, I almost died. You can't ask me to do that again, not again, please. I don't want to die yet. I just got my brother back, and you are asking me to throw my life away, or worse still, to throw him back into the same death trap from which we just saved him. No, No!"

Andy, who had not spoken since their conversation began, and who looked like he hadn't heard a single word they were saying, got off his seat and walked up to his sister. Taking her hand in his, he spoke softly.

"You won't have to do everything alone this time, we'll do it together. You don't have to be afraid either; you will have me by your side all through the journey. Together, we can achieve this. We can free the divine warriors together," he said. His words reassured her, although a modicum of fear could still be seen on her face, but she took some courage from his courage and tried to snipe away at her own fears. It was only right that they reciprocate Methira's goodness.

"How do we do this?" Josie asked, turning to Methira.

"First thing we must do is find my people. I will need your help with finding them. With my people, we can cause a distraction powerful enough to get Dromos out of his lair. When this happens, you both can sneak into his inner sanctum and retrieve the four golden boxes holding the Four Divine Warriors. This has to be our first move."

They watched her as she spoke, nodding their heads to all that the fairy queen was saying. It made perfect sense; they could not be able to sneak into Dromos' lair unless they were first able to distract him. His powers were too strong to be taken head on. Their best system of approach would be to come in from his blind side and surprise him completely. Josie's fears were already melting away like wax before fire, and she had her hand still held tight in her brother's hand.

"Where do we begin the search?" She asked, looking straight at Methira who smiled for the first time since they met.

CHAPTER TWO

FOR WHAT SEEMED LIKE AN ETERNITY, NONE of the three travelers said a word to each other; all that could be heard in the haunted woods they traveled through was the charred, deathly ruins of a once blossoming kingdom, Mytherios.

The smell of rotten wood filled the air about them, and scarcely would anyone pass through that forest without sensing the anger of wandering, unsung souls. The night was blanketed in a grey mist that seemed to have a mind of its own, and more than once did Josie and Andy find themselves groping for support as their legs locked onto a root sticking out unnaturally.

"This forest seems to be interested in taking our lives at all cost," Josie let out as she rose from a fall. Her hair was a dragnet of dried leaves, and her clothes were soiled from cleaning her hands on them every time something brought her down.

"I didn't want to be the one to say it," said Andy. He blew at his bruised palm.

"The mist is not really a mist," said Methira. "It is a cloud of the countless fairy souls that have nowhere to go to. The entire forest is filled with the anger of these homeless souls."

"Aren't fairies supposed to be nice? These ones are simply trying to kill us," Andy grumbled.

"Andy!" Josie exclaimed.

The fairy queen raised a hand. "Oh, please, do let him be," she said, "you are right, Andy. Fairies are indeed kind spirits. But when you have no place to call home… some things begin to snap within you, with the part that makes you nice breaking first."

Andy stared long into Methira's flaming eyes, and somehow, he understood. When Dromos had held him captive, he felt so helpless, so vulnerable, and it was frustrating. A frustration that became a fit of broiling anger within him.

They arrived at what looked like a clearing. Methira heaved beside them. This particular clearing used to be a magical garden for children; it had plants that would sing when touched and creatures that would dance to the melody; she could still hear the playful screams of the young fairies. It used to be the safest place in the world, until Dromos. All was fine until Dromos happened, and then it became a grave of smiles and dreams.

"Come," Methira said to Josie and Andy, "Let me show you something."

She led them through the forest to the edge of the woodlands. Fighting off life-threatening trees and the living mist, they made their way through to the edge of the woods.

"Is this…" Andy pointed to the vast and empty grasslands and mountains before them, "…is this what you wanted to show us? This is just a woodless version of the forest," he said, "Dromos' destruction is all that is left here."

Before them was an endless array of grasses and little mountains the shape of a snail's shell. In the midst of the grassland stood two fairy statues standing a hundred feet away from each other. The statues themselves were like even smaller versions of the mountains.

They had their four stone wings spread in all directions behind them. Each statue stretched forward on one foot, like children frozen during a walk. They both raised a hand to the sky like they were cupping golden waters from an unseen spring pouring down from the sky.

"Methira, we will help you release the four warriors and liberate your people," Josie assured, unable to make anything of the emptiness before her.

The fairy queen only smiled at this. "Look at the wasteland before you," she said to them. "Hear its eerie quietness and remember its depressing emptiness. I have something else to show you."

Josie and Andy nodded and took another look around. The mountains in their view looked like evil stone giants frozen in time; about them was grassland with grasses a few shades darker than the usual green. In the vast distance, they heard the echoes of beasts howling.

Methira spread her golden wings behind her, and they gave a faint flicker. "I can only do what I am about to do for a short moment. If my fairy light is left on for too long, Dromos will find us."

Her wings began to flap behind her, and she lifted off the ground with the ease of a feather in a light wind. "Close your eyes and clear your minds," she said to the siblings. They obeyed and shut their eyes in an instant, holding their hands and bracing themselves for whatever was coming their way.

It felt like a hypnic jerk, as if they were falling off a cliff at an incredible speed. Josie and Andy felt their legs lift off the ground. Were they levitating? The urge to open their eyes and see what was happening tore through them like electricity, but they somehow managed to keep their eyes closed. The next few minutes were like a walk through a storm – terrific.

"You can open your eyes now." They exhaled in relief when Methira said this to them.

Their eyes opened slowly, like shy flowers yielding to the morning sun.

Before they closed their eyes, the fields and the grasses spoke of a forgotten past, a wretched present, and a doomed future. But the meadow that stood before them now was different; it was... alive. The grasses bore a cascade of colors: bright yellow, blue, red, gold...some colors had no names, but the most amazing fact about them was that they were singing and dancing.

The two fairy statues had a carpet of green leaves covering them. In the hands that they raised were either ends of a slight arc – a small rainbow.

Josie and Andy gasped when they saw this. Then came fairies from a cave at the foot of one of the small mountains. The older fairies were golden and silver in colour, but with such sparkle, each one shone like a glittering crystal. The younger ones bore different colors: blue, pink, red, green, and white.

Something snapped and flashed, and the paradise before them closed up like a book.

The siblings said nothing to Methira. They tried to, but the words wouldn't come. Josie mustered courage and met Methira's eyes. They were soft with tears and crimson with pain, the pain of having to what your past looked like and to have to live in the horror that the present and future had become.

"I am sorry, Methira," Andy said, "I did not understand your pain before, and even now, I do not understand it, but at least I know what its shadows look like..." He walked to Methira and held her in a warm embrace.

Even though not a single day had passed without the fairy queen mourning the destruction of her people, she still could not hold back the tears that poured down her face when Andy embraced her. In that instant, the wounds from her past were forced open and refreshed again.

Andy broke the embrace slowly. "Wipe your tears, Methira. They will be the last you ever shed for your people." He closed his eyes, heaved, opened them again, and continued, "I will help you free your people, even if it costs me my life."

"Andy, don't make promises you can't keep; no harm must befall you!" Josie cried.

Methira sniffed and wiped at her tears. "Your sister is right, Andy," she said in her soft yet commanding voice, "you should not make such promises. You have your life to live." Andy looked from Josie to Methira and from Methira back to Josie.

"No, I am not making a promise," he said, "I am only telling you my plans. Now let's hurry and be on our way. We have a lair to break into. And so saying, he set off, leaving the two ladies rushing to catch up with him.

Andy led the way now, standing ahead and looking around at the slightest sound. A root tripped him and all he said was, "Don't worry, root, we will soon make you happy again."

As they continued on their journey, the mist seemed to clear the path ahead and then close up behind them like a curtain. "Is it just me, or has the forest stopped attacking us?" Josie asked.

Methira looked around and nodded in agreement. "They sense our mission, what we are going to do, and they are reacting to it."

"They want to be free," Josie remarked.

"Yes, despite the layers of darkness covering their souls now, they are still alive, deep inside, and sometimes, that is all that is necessary."

"I fear for him," Josie said to Methira, "I don't want anything to hurt him."

"You won't always be there for him, Josie," Methira replied, "It is best to teach him how to live life without you."

"No, I will always be there for him," Josie snapped angrily.

"You weren't there with him in Dromos's lair."

Josie stood in front of Methira and turned around sharply. "Well, I am now."

"I know. There was, however, an instance when you were not, and he did well without you."

Josie was about to reply to Methira when a sharp cackle resounded around.

Methira's eyes widened in recognition. "He is here," she muttered and ran forward.

Andy had a wooden stake in his hand.

"Where did you find that?" Josie asked when she raced to his side.

He shrugged his shoulders. "Turns out the forest is also an armory."

"Show yourself, Dark Goblin, I know you are here," Methira ordered. Her eyes were balls of lightning flashing in their sockets.

A small evil laugh came from the dark space ahead of them. Two green, oval eyes turned around in the darkness.

"Oh, Methira, still as fierce as always," The Dark Goblin said. He fell into a cackle that sounded like the laughter of a hyena. "Tell me," he began, floating slowly to where they stood, "how did you feel when Lord Dromos sent his minion to rip your lands to shreds and death? How did you feel then?" Methira said nothing.

"Of course, you were silent then, just like you are now," taunted The Dark Goblin. "Silent and helpless—"

"She is not helpless, we are going to stand by her, you ugly goblin," Andy interposed. He stepped forward.

The Dark Goblin bent over in laughter. "My name is Taurus. I know that Lord Dromos has a taste for human pie. I just did not expect the queen of the fairies to offer him fillings."

"Be silent now, Taurus," Josie retorted with a flash of fury.

He gave a low growl and made to advance but changed his mind midway. "I plan to defeat Lord Dromos."

The siblings gasped.

"I see you are impressed, however, that is only a step in my grand scheme, I plan to rule over Mytherios when that happens."

"Oh really? You just had to ruin it!" retorted Andy.

"What?! Ruin what?!"

"Never mind," Andy replied with a wave of the hand, "but I must warn you, your ambition will come to fruition in Neverland. Only in Neverland."

"You have grown mad, Taurus," Methira cooed, "And do you think I will let you bring your dark goblins into the land of the fairies? Impossible."

"It would have been impossible if the fairies still lived in the land, but as things stand, Lord Dromos rules over Mytherios, and that means whoever gets Dromos gets Mytherios. It is a very open game. Or do you not agree?" he growled menacingly.

"Get behind me!" Methira shouted to the siblings. If they had been a second late, they would have been burned by the flaming green ball Taurus threw. Methira blanked out after this.

Andy growled and charged. Josie supported her brother on the other flank. But Taurus, the dark lord of the goblins, only laughed at this.

"See you later," he said as he vanished into thin air with the same cackle.

Andy was about to return to Methira's side when he noticed a shape in the dull moonlight flying towards them.

"We have company," he announced to his sister.

"No," Methira's voice squeaked through, "She is a fairy, one of my sisters. One of the last fairies."

The said fairy landed. She was taller than Methira and was coated in black.

"Long time no see, Spektra," Methira said.

"Long time no see, sister," Spektra replied as she threw herself around Methira.

CHAPTER THREE

FAR BEYOND THE DESOLATE WOODLANDS OF MYTHERIOS, beyond its darkened borders and the reach of its undead mist, beyond the shadows of its small mountains, towards the sinking of the sun, lay a land characterized by the screams of spirits, monsters, fairies, trolls, and humans long perished, but still howling about Dromos as his slaves.

The first thing felt by anyone who visited that place would be the unseen chill that caused the blood to recoil into the heart. And then the smell of man's ancient enemy – death – and the countless skulls and remains of many fallen.

If one's heart somehow did not explode in anxiety and fear, and one continued into this land with its sky and its stormy clouds threatening to rain hell which never let down a drop, one would find a lone path: The Lane of the

Undead, adorned on either side with what was left of those that had rebelled against Dromos.

A mountain whose peak speared several thousand feet high towards the north stood at the end of the Lane of the Undead. A stair spiraled about this mountain, and halfway to its top was a cave the size of a small kingdom. One would find people that were dead and forgotten, armed with swords, but yet screaming for release. In this surreal kingdom of whispering souls and demonic monstrosities ruled Dromos.

The monsters that bowed before Dromos, lord of the Underworld, were all fidgety. And why not? The thing about falling on the wrong side of the lord of the Underworld's favor was that not even death was an escape. There was no running away. No, there was no escaping death, unless of course you should obtain the favor of the God of Light and somehow did not end up in the Underworld.

Dromos would walk the length of the cave, turn around, and his underlings would shake like reeds on a stream. Suddenly, he would sit on his throne again, and in less than a minute, jump up and resume his patrol of fury.

"Tell me, Ratifi," Dromos thundered from his throne, an ugly bulk hewn crudely out of the mountain, "tell me where the human siblings are."

The four-armed, half-orc, half-goblin whimpered. "I—I will find them Lord Dromos," he said. He had small eyes spaced out all over his body.

"And how do you intend to do that?!" The lord of the Underworld growled with such ferocity that the walls began to tremble.

Ratifi raised his head and quickly resumed his task of boring a hole into the cave floor with his stare. "I have eyes scattered abroad…"

Someone or something behind stifled a laugh. "There's something about…pardon the double entendre, my friend, but there's something about you scattering your eyes abroad…I mean, aren't they scattered about your body?"

"What are you doing here?" Dromos hissed.

"I am Taurus, lord of the dark goblins at your service," Taurus said, bowing with a flourish as he did.

Dromos raised his head enquiringly.

"I have learned of your many conquests and victories, and I am here to pledge my unscattered loyalty to you," Taurus bowed again.

"And why should we believe you?" asked Ratifi, "Last time you were not much help, and you left me for dead."

Taurus scoffed at this. "There is no *we* between you and Lord Dromos, scattered man, and it doesn't matter if I am an enemy or not, I would never be able to defeat the lord of the Underworld."

"Fine," said Dromos, "Be assured, however, that if you displease me, I will give your head to the war dogs and your soul to my undead."

"War dogs, undead, all is as clear as the sun," Taurus said, bowing again.

Ratifi growled within himself. He made no attempt to hide the hate he had for the newcomer.

"Ratifi," Dromos called, pulling him out of his reverie, "take an army of undead and find me those human siblings."

"Yes, my lord," he replied and turned to leave. His voice shook with foreboding. "If you return without them, then I will ensure you leave without your head."

Without turning back, Ratifi gave a slight bow and departed from the cave.

Dromos turned to Taurus. "Ratifi might be a stupid, four-armed reptile with eyes scattered abroad, but he is my most loyal servant. And yet, you disgraced him before me."

Taurus gave a nervous chuckle. "Oh, I did not mean to…"

Dromos raised a ringed finger. "Be silent," he said with a dangerous calm. "I hope for your sake, and the sake of your people, dark lord of the goblins, that you do not disappoint me."

"Oh well, in that case, I do have something to say," the goblin chortled, desperation seeping into his voice.

"And what would that be?"

"You have to promise me something first…"

"I do not have the time for games, speak…"

"Ah-ah, I know my life is worth no more than a game to you, but you see, my lord, this game is all I have, your word first."

"What do you want?"

"A place by your side."

"Granted, now speak."

"I know where the human siblings are."

Dromos's eyes flashed a bright red flame. "You do?"

"Ah-ah, yes Lord Dromos," he replied. "I saw them making their way out of Mytherios, and there's a little bit of surprise there…"

Dromos stared at the goblin with narrowed eyes. "No, no, that is impossible."

"Ah-ah, but it happened, I saw it with my eyes."

"She perished with her people."

"No, she did not," said Taurus, "the fairy queen, Methira is still very much alive."

Dromos heaved; an evil smile crept into his face. "It is a pleasant surprise indeed," he said. "Two rare human children and a vanquished queen would be a fine collection. Go and join Ratifi and tell him all the words that you have said to me now."

"Yes, my lord," Taurus bowed.

"And join Ratifi in the hunt for those slippery customers."

Taurus found Ratifi in The Valley of the Dead. His eyes were closed, all of them, and his lips quivered in senseless mumblings. He was there, and yet, somehow, he was not there.

The dark goblin lord encircled Ratifi, examining the huge serpent more closely this time. He tried to count the eyes scattered all over the serpent, but he never got past a hundred before he had to start all over again.

"Ratifi?" he called, "Ratifi!"

He gritted his teeth, a scattered row of small, brown bones. "Stupid snake, always stupid. But he is no snake, is he?" Taurus said to no one at all, sniffing around the entranced serpent's hands. "What snake has four arms?"

A chilly wind blew from across the valley: the wind of the vale. The Valley of the Dead was where the Underworld came closest to Earth. Many times, when the veil between the two worlds was weak, determined and strong demons would break through the veil from the Underworld and would unleash such unimaginable on the unthinking civilization they visited first.

The Valley of the Dead would have been no different from any other valley or desert really; it never rained in The Valley of the Dead, and the sun's light never got that far. The entire place was lit instead by the flames of the Underworld burning through the cracks that ran everywhere like a million snakes on a rampage.

When Dromos first appeared, he did through here, and it was at this very place that he summoned his army. The Army of the Undead.

The problem with fighting Dromos was that every soul he killed became his to summon. If he killed ten men, it simply meant that he had recruited ten men to his Army of the Undead. The only chance anybody had at bringing him down was to confront him to the face, which was tantamount to suicide itself.

Overwhelmed by impatience and idleness, Taurus stood from the small rock he had sat on for what seemed to be an eternity. His back was bent like an old man, bent almost to a hunch. He stretched a hand and reached for Ratifi's face.

"I wouldn't do that, goblin," Ratifi spoke. His eyes flew open with the darting speed of a snake's tongue.

"I am no ordinary goblin," Taurus snapped, rising to his feet. He had been so startled by Ratifi's sudden return to life that he staggered backward and fell on his small, flat buttocks, hard.

"That is none of my concern," Ratifi replied. Apart from his eyes that flew open and the small movements of his mouth as he spoke, there was no other sign his body was not a carved statue.

"Why are you here, staring out into nothing?"

"I was never here," Ratifi replied. He turned his head, so his gaze met with the goblin's, "I have just arrived," he said.

Taurus waved in dismissal. "Oh, I get it now," he said, "you were meditating,"

"I was not meditating," Ratifi began, "I traveled to the Underworld to summon the undead army; they will help in the search."

"You cannot find two humans and a powerless queen yourself?"

Ratifi scoffed. "One would expect a goblin to make up for the ridiculously small size with an exceptional brain at least."

"You had to say that much…?"

"Mytherios is a very large place for one being to comb, but our large number would mean we get to cover more ground in the same time."

"I am coming with you," Taurus announced.

"No, I refuse."

"I wasn't asking you; I was informing you."

"I will not allow you to do that…"

"You will disobey Lord Dromos's order?"

Ratifi stuttered at this. "How do I know that you are telling the truth? Why should I believe you?"

"Your faith or rather, the lack of it, is none of my concern," Taurus chipped. "If you are so desperate for an answer, you could meditate your way to Lord Dromos."

Ratifi let out a low growl. He heaved. "Fine," he said, "but the prisoners are mine. If you do as much as touch a strand of hair on their heads, I will gut you…"

A sigh escaped Taurus's lips. "…such kind thoughts…"

"… and spread your insides against the rocks."

The floor beneath them shook.

"What is that?" Taurus asked. His eyes darted wildly about.

Ratifi smiled, content to see the goblin disoriented. "That… is the undead army; the force of Lord Dromos." He raised his arms, all four of them thickly built, to the sky and cackled.

The cracks in the floor began to widen. Then, a sound like the cry of an agonized multitude, blared through the valley. Ratifi reveled in the sound. Taurus hid from it.

Soon, they began to crawl out: men the color of phantoms, mindless and endless in their count

"Are they really necessary?" Taurus asked.

"How about you go ask Lord Dromos. I am sure he will be obliged to react to your foolishness," Ratifi replied, grateful for the chance to hit back at Taurus for his remarks earlier.

"Ah, a neck offering advice. I will pass on this one, thank you."

Ratifi turned around to face Taurus. "Tell me again why I shouldn't kill you right now."

Taurus scratched his head with a finger.

"Because Lord Dromos sent me?"

"He doesn't even know you. Why do you think he will miss you?" asked Ratifi. He was approaching Taurus now, an *I-will-kill-you-painfully* a smile flitted across his face.

"That's right," Taurus replied with an air of unconcern, "I think I remember why now."

"Why?"

"Because I know where the humans and the queen are, and you don't."

Ratifi growled. "Very well," he said, "remember, they are all mine. Not yours at all."

"Oh, I really pity the queen and those little rats she's moving about with. They don't know what's coming for them."

CHAPTER FOUR

EVEN THOUGH IT WAS ONLY EVENING, THE WOOD creaked with an uncanny silence. And beyond the snap of fallen branches and the crunch of dried leaves under the feet of the travelers, there was an amount of unnatural voices echoing through everywhere.

You didn't have to be there when Dromos swept through the once-golden woods of Mytherios like seven coalesced plagues to feel the death hanging in the air. The sun was behind them now, bathing the woods in a last rush of golden light and friendliness. When the night takes over the sky, the memories of that dark day will haunt the restless souls again, and they'd fall back into their hateful snare.

"Are we getting closer to the mountains at all?" Andy asked. He had led the party before, but the fatigue was getting to him, and he was becoming as snappish as the forest they traversed. "At this rate we will never find any other fairy before I'm a hundred."

"Now, we wouldn't be moving if we weren't getting any closer, isn't that right?" Spektra replied. She preferred flying. If only those humans had wings, they'd be halfway there by now. But there was also an equal amount of chance that they'd be spotted and shot down before they even got to the lonely path.

"I thought about it too," Methira said to Spektra, "We have to find the other surviving fairies before Dromos or his army does."

"You thought about what?" asked Josie. Her hair was matted together like dried papier-mâché with a fair number of tiny leaves and branches in it.

"Flying."

"We'd be shot down before we even got half-way, Dromos can notice a flying fairy from a hundred leagues away," Spektra said in disagreement. Dromos could sense their magic when they took flight and track its scent like a bloodhound. Heavens be with whatever creature that led him there.

"We need all hands if we are to survive this one battle, humans included," Methira said as she jumped over a fallen log. Even though her hair had gone through the same treatment as Josie's, its golden tresses still looked beautiful. It seemed that having magic had its pros and cons.

A bird in a tree nearby gave a loud wail.

"It is very funny that you guys should need humans," Andy chirped, "the all-powerful fairies need puny humans to save their home. Even I find it ridiculous."

"Andy!" Josie cried, upset.

"It's alright." Methira chuckled. He had always amused her, that Andy boy. He had fire and passion in him. And that was why he, more often than not, would wind up saying something his sister found appalling.

"Lord Dromos and his cohorts know too much about us," Spektra began, "how we think, fight…" she choked on her words, "…or try to… and all. So, we are old news to them. But you siblings are a different matter altogether."

Josie spoke again. "What do you mean?" she asked.

Methira cleared her throat. "Fairies are a long-time acquaintance of the Underworld, which explains why they know how and when to attack."

"Not that any other form of attack would have failed though," Josie noted. "Fairies have never had to fight."

Spektra threw a glance at Methira. "Our generation did not learn to fight, but the fairies before us wielded magic with purposes that went beyond putting a smile on people's faces."

"I wish they didn't," said Methira. "Dromos is a direct consequence of their magical overzealousness."

"What do you mean?" Andy asked. He sat at the foot of a dead birch, "The fairies and Dromos have history?"

"Yes," Methira replied, "Legend has it that the earlier fairies were not cruel, but they are not as harmless as we were either. So, when Dromos's race attacked, they were all wiped out, every last one of them. Dromos was a young prince then, and he swore to avenge his people."

"From the look of things, I'd say he's done a dark job," Andy said. He picked up a small, dried branch from the forest floor. "I have a question to ask," he said to Methira.

"Andy," Josie called, her voice warning him not to say anything rash.

"Ask, but do not be insensitive, please," Methira said. Her usually bright eyes had clouds as dark as the fast-approaching night gathered in them.

"What are you going to do when you meet Dromos? Are you going to kill him?"

Spektra snickered. Her body shone a bright red. "Is that even a question?" she asked. There was a cutting edge in her voice. "He killed our people: children, women, men, our homes, and he just took all of that away from us, I'll kill him the moment I have the chance," she raved.

"Isn't that what the earlier fairies did to his people, too?" asked Josie, as she took a seat beside her brother.

"They attacked first," Spektra replied hotly. "Obliteration was the only possible outcome."

"Right now, don't you wish obliteration isn't the only thing on Dromos's mind?" Andy chimed.

An overwhelming silence crawled on them.

Spektra bit her lower lip and sat on the root of a tree. The tree, like the others here, had roots that stuck out of the ground up to knee length and were sometimes two-feet wide.

"We will camp here for the night to allow you kids some rest," she announced.

"I am sure I won't be sleeping a wink tonight," Andy declared. "These trees look like they have a jaw hidden somewhere."

Methira chuckled. "These are strictly herbal trees; they can't eat you." But the trees weren't strictly herbal trees. They used to be one of the little fairies' favorites because the branches moved when you sat on them. But Methira didn't want to say that; she was tired of remembering a past that was so perfect and yet nothing more than a memory now.

They couldn't risk starting a fire; darkness was all that was left of the woods of Mytherios. If Dromos's hounds saw any form of light in these sides, they'd be here in no time, angry and bloodthirsty. Instead, Methira and Spektra combined their magics and cast a warming spell round the kids who were already snoring.

"Do you think he is right," Spektra asked her sister. Her eyes reflected the tiny twinkles up in the night sky. "that we are no better than Dromos ourselves?"

"Oh, we are a million times better than Dromos," Methira said.

"But we wiped out their race, just like ours is on the brink of extinction now."

"We did not wipe out their race. The early fairies did that, and there is nothing we desired more than a world where we did not have to learn how to defend ourselves. A world where sword and bloodshed were a myth. That is what we desired. All we ever desired."

Spektra sighed, relieved.

"Andy is right about one thing though," said Methira. "We are moving too slowly. We will have to risk flying if we want to cover any real distance.

The next morning, Methira announced to the kids that they'd have to fly into the mountains.

"And get shot out of the sky like a duck? Thank you, but I'll pass," said Andy.

Josie rubbed her face. "Did you not say that Dromos could sense you from far away and that flying makes it easier for his army to find us? What is this I'm hearing now?"

"It reduces during the day," Methira replied. "Our light and its magic makes it easier to trace us at night, but during the day, you have to be close to trace our magic."

Andy stared at Spektra. Hesitation loomed about his eyes. "You know, maybe trekking is not such a bad idea."

"Andy, come over here. Spektra will take Josie."

Josie whimpered. "Can't I come with you instead?"

Methira cupped Josie's small white face in her hands. "You will be alright, I promise," She assured.

The fairies stepped behind the children and wrapped their arms firmly about the kids' waists. Methira spread her golden wings and Spektra spread her black, beautiful ones. With a cry, they took off into the morning skies.

The kids screamed in ecstasy as they were borne into the bright yellow sky by two royal fairies, relics of a ravaged world. When the fairies saw that the kids were thrilled, they decided to put on a show. They soared into the skies, the clouds beneath them looked like they were on fire. After which, they let themselves fall back to the ground before taking to the air again, a few feet from falling to their deaths.

As they edged closer to the mountains however, the peaceful blue skies turned an angry black, and the wind that had kissed against their faces threatened to blow them off the surface of the earth. Then, out of nowhere, a vengeful rain started. Instead of drops, it came down in bucketfuls, and when they splashed, the scattered sprays stung their eyes like shards of broken glass.

In spite of their magic, the fairies heaved in relief when the valley between the two mountains became visible. It was said that a number of survivors still lurked about the mountains. They quickly landed and made for a small cave. Methira's eyes darted around furiously, almost like she was seeing something no one else could see, and it was Josie who noticed this.

"Methira, are you alright?" she asked slipping her hand in the fairy's whiter hand.

Methira gave a chuckle that was torn between looking like a smile and coming off as a grin. Eventually, it took on the shape of a face trying to hide secrets. "I am fine child," she said. "Do not worry about me."

Josie was about to say something in protest when the storm stopped just as suddenly as it started. The rain stopped as abruptly as well, as if the sky had suddenly ran out of tears to shed.

The company stepped out of their hiding spot onto the wet grass of the valley between the mountains.

"That's strange," said Andy.

Spektra nodded in agreement. "In all my three-hundred years of existence I have never seen such rain."

"Uh, yes, the rain is strange, but there's something stranger up there, and it is coming straight at us," the boy whimpered.

As if on cue, the rest of the party turned around to see the intruder. Spektra braced, a covering of scales began to shield her body.

"Nice amour," Andy commented.

Methira on the other hand was stoic, almost as if she was expecting whatever was coming.

The green and yellow comet heading towards them fell some ten feet away, spreading a strange mist of yellow and green around it. Surprisingly, there was no noise, almost like it had never touched the ground. As the mist cleared, the outline of a figure – a woman with wings – came into view.

Andy and the others stepped aside as Methira made her way forward. The figure stepped out of the mist and came into view. It was a woman who almost looked like Methira.

"That… is beautiful…" Andy said, gaping.

Annoyed, Josie pushed his lower jaw upwards. "Don't be a pervert," she said.

The figure had stood face to face with Methira now. "Long time no see, Methira."

"Solana!" Methira cried. She ran forward and threw a hand over the newcomer's neck. The two of them remained that way, locked around each other's necks for a while.

"I thought you were dead!" Methira squealed when they broke their embrace.

"I thought I was going to die," Solana replied, then looked behind Methira and greeted the rest of the company. "We were going to keep fighting, and perhaps, we might have won too," Solana recalled, "But then Dromos sent Ratifi and a fresh horde of his undead army. And that's when I knew it was time to retreat. I made it across Mytherios with a handful of others."

Methira's eyes widened. "There are others?"

Solana smiled. "And they can't wait to be reunited with their queen."

CHAPTER FIVE

"WHAT IN THE DWARF'S BEARD IS THAT STORM THERE?" Taurus, dark lord of the goblins shrieked, pointing at the storm gathered about the twin mountains of Vohra.

"That is a storm, goblin idiot," Ratifi retorted with a scowl. He hated the weasel Dromos had asked him to work with. A slimy creature was what he was; the type that went behind you to plan your death. He loathed him and wouldn't mind knocking a few of his already sparse dental elements out.

"I know," Taurus balked. He stared at the half reptile, half orc, half only-the-Lord-of-Light-knows-what talking back at him. Speaking of proportion, three halves did not add up to one; he knew that. He was smart. But the giant with tiny eyes scattered all over his body was big enough to make one and a half. It was a good thing he had a few tricks up his claws.

"If you know, then why are you asking?" Ratifi retorted, his voice having a sneer to it, "I thought you goblins were supposed to make up in brains what you lacked in size."

Taurus sniveled. "Well, if you must know, that storm was conjured by the witch."

"The witch is dead," Ratifi said as a matter-of-factly, "She died a long time ago."

"Ah," Taurus scoffed. His rat-like oil spot eyes bulged as he spoke, "No one is ever truly dead. As the commander of an undead army, I would have expected you to know that much."

Ratifi stopped in his tracks and the stomping of the thousand undead souls marching behind him ceased. A disturbing silence ran across the entire forest. "One of these days, I am going to cut off your head and have it impaled on a spear and carried before me, so whoever sees it would learn to fear me, if they want to keep their heads."

The dark goblin doubled over and laughed. With water in his eyes, he said, "It wouldn't be you that they fear then. It'd be the head of the terrible dark lord of the goblins that the people you talk about would fear. They'd say, "even in his death, the Dark Goblin still leads mighty Ratifi to battle."

A red fury erupted within Ratifi, and he would probably have struck Taurus if the latter had not reminded him that they had a fairy and two slippery siblings to catch, and that Dromos would not wait forever.

With a groan, Ratifi changed his mind and said instead, "when this is over, you and I will meet somewhere that allows two beings to walk in but only being to walk out alive."

"I'll be looking forward to it," he said, swallowing as he did.

Ratifi turned to face his army. The entire forest was lit by the ghostly green light shining off their bodies. They were humans once. Now they were just souls that wanted to rest. "The soul that finds Methira and the human children will be allowed to return to the Underworld. Now all of you, march on and find me my prizes." He stared hard at Taurus as he said the last parts.

With a groan, the undead army lunged forward. The earth shook under their feet and great clouds of dust swept up behind them.

"What's that noise?" asked Josie.

Methira's eyes were closed with the soberness of a meditating monk. Then without a warning, they snapped open. "I sense a dark energy. Not one, but many entities joined together by a single dark energy.

"So far, we know that there is only one person capable of doing that," Solana said.

Methira shook her head like someone who can't believe the dream they called a nightmare has been their life the whole time. There was something to pity about her. Walking to your own death for a greater good is a hard choice to make, but being hunted down by an enemy you stand almost no chance against was a different height to scale altogether, even for a fairy queen — especially for a fairy queen.

"Wait here," Methira ordered. There was something in her voice that reminded the rest of the party that she was the queen of the fairies. They nodded in obedience. She took to the sky and flew towards the edge of the mountain. Her eyes perused the forest around her. Nothing was in sight, or was there? In the distance towards the west, dust gathered like a desert storm and rose to the sky. She stared harder and that's when she saw it, the source of the energy they had felt earlier, the undead army was here.

If the undead were here, then Dromos had to be nearby. Otherwise, the savage creature that purged her people with fire had to be leading. They were the only ones who could lead the undead souls into battle.

After her quick reconnaissance, Methira hurried back to the company, to tell them of the fresh dangers they were in, not that they were ever out of danger anyway. But they had been the ones heading for their demise, chasing after freedom like an elf's arrow would chase after its mark. Now danger was chasing them, and the bondage it brought was not too far behind.

Spektra stepped forward. "We must leave," she said.

"She is right, Methira, we must leave," Solana assented.

But Methira only shook her head. "If I do that then I will be putting all of us in danger."

They understood. One thing about fairy magic was that you could create new worlds within the existing worlds in it. You could cause water to be sweet and fire to be no warmer than a bowl of soup. And then, there was also the aspect of it being so unique that it was equally easy to follow, but it disappeared fast too. However, Methira doubted it'd disappear fast enough this time around.

Methira took a deep breath and exhaled. "I have to stay back and fend them off," she announced.

"That's not a very good decision," said Andy.

"Methira, they will capture you for sure!" Josie cried. Her eyes were wet with tears now.

Solana understood what Methira was trying to do. The children at least had to be saved and the rest warned about what was coming their way.

"I will stay with you," said Solana, "we will do this together."

But Methira was also shaking her head in protest. "You cannot die now; you exposed yourself for my sake."

Solana chortled. Suddenly, a bright light flashed through her body. And when it disappeared, she was looking prepared for whatever was to come. Unlike Spektra, whose armor was made of scale-like plates lining over each other, Solana's armor was a joining of green leaf shaped plates and a yellow sun running in the middle.

"Who said anything about dying?" She replied to Methira, "And I am not dying for you, I am dying for the Queen of Mytherios and her people—my people."

Andy turned aside to Josie and whispered: "Isn't that the same thing that Methira said? In different words though."

"Spektra," Methira called, "you will have to find a safe place for them," she nodded towards Josie and Andy, "Solana and I will stop those undead from advancing any further."

Spektra bowed, then turned to Solana. "How do I find the others?"

"They will find you," Solana replied, "Now get out of here, it is about to rain fire and undead souls."

And fairies. Josie thought but never said it out loud.

Spektra spread out her wings and grabbed Josie and Andy with each hand. She turned to face Methira one last time and said, "Be safe my lady."

The fairy queen deigned no response to this request. She was about to face an army of undead souls. The last time that happened, all of her kingdom vanished in the battle, and now, she was going to do it again, with an army of one.

"Wait!" Methira said to Spektra and then turned to Solana, "The survivors would never find them Solana, they don't even know that they exist."

Solana bit her lower lip at this.

Methira's eyes sparked and then began to glow.

"What are you doing?!" Solana yelled. Hot tears gathered in her eyes. She had just met her queen after so long a time, why did she have to lose her immediately?

"I am giving you a chance to escape," Methira said. The words were barely out of her mouth when a magical wall stretched out of her body and across the mountains.

"Go now!"

Solana hesitated.

"Go Solana!"

With a cry, Solana and Spektra lifted Josie and Andy, rocketing out of the valley into the listless sky above them.

Methira had hoped that the next time she and Dromos would meet it wouldn't be like old times. He had nearly obliterated them then. She had hoped that the next fight was going to be different; that they'd be fairies, not colorful, harmless butterflies. *Oh, this is the end,* she thought.

Ratifi and Taurus marched into the valley just as Solana and Spektra took to the sky. In a moment of rage and foolishness, Ratifi ran after them, or at least he was going to until he ran into the barrier Methira had put up.

The force of the barrier threw him twenty feet backwards. He staggered to his feet with a stunned look on his face.

Taurus, the dark goblin snickered. "All brawns no brains," he muttered, although he was careful to ensure Ratifi did not hear what he said.

Ratifi growled and charged again. This time, heading directly for the fairy queen, but this attempt was twice as bad a decision as the first. And he stumbled some forty feet backwards, tumbling into an ugly pile. "What are you staring at?" he yelled. "Attack the barrier, tear it down!" he grimaced.

Taurus stood aside watching the entire scene with the air of an accomplished sage.

The undead soldiers' attempt at tearing down the barrier could be summed up in three words: Ratifi fared better.

He grimaced. Watching the fairy queen on the other side and being unable to do anything was a different kind of torture to him.

Suddenly, there was a crack behind the undead army and a portal opened above them.

Dromos emerged from the portal as the undead bowed and hurrie out of his path. Ratifi and Taurus did the same. He let out a low growl.

"Who do we have here?" he taunted. "Is this not the vanquished princess of the fairies?"

He walked to the edge of the barrier and chuckled. His cold stare fell on Ratifi.

"Have you been unable to bring her because of... this?" he pointed at the barrier.

Ratifi cowered in shame and defeat. To survive under Dromos, one of the things he learned was to bow.

Dromos turned his attention to Methira who was having a hard time keeping the barrier up now. "Your cheap tricks will not save you from me this time." And so saying, he curled his hand into a fist and with a roar rammed at the barrier.

At first, nothing happened, but Methira knew better. Then the barrier cracked in all directions like dried clay. A loud shatter followed, and the barrier broke down, smashing into a thousand and one tiny pieces.

Methira, exhausted already from holding up the barrier, simply could not withstand the force of her barrier being torn apart and she fell to the ground, unconscious.

A satisfied grin played across Dromos face. "It has only just begun, Methira."

Taurus hurried forward. "The kids were taken by other fairies, two of them."

Dromos exhaled, his nose flaring like a dragon's. "From now on, I will lead the assault. There will be no surviving or escaping my wrath. On to victory!"

He stomped forward, his undead army marching closely behind to hunt every last fairy that ever existed.

CHAPTER SIX

ANDY AND JOSIE COULD ONLY WATCH METHIRA get captured by Dromos. They had never in all their lives felt as weak as they did in that fateful moment. It was a huge setback, and it gave them more questions they needed answers for.

How did they get here? Would there ever be a point where the odds favored them? Or was trying to restore Mytherios a long road to nowhere? Instead of seeking freedom, why were they running for survival now?

It is incredulous how quickly tables turn. And not just incredulous but agonizing too. How things can escalate quickly from worse to far worse. If life gives you lemons, you make lemonade, but what happens when life gives you rotten lemons?

The two fairies, Spektra and Solana, bore Josie and Andy in their hands as they went higher into the clouds, their wings folding and opening like large pages of a book.

To the ordinary observer, the fairies had to deal with only the weight of the children they each carried. But a more careful look into matters would reveal that they also had to bear another weight, unless the grief of leaving their queen to deal with the same force that had wiped out most of their kind was no weight at all.

Spektra tried to concentrate, but she couldn't. As a black fairy, her duty was to do all the things that weren't fit for a fairytale. She was a warrior, a soldier sworn to protect the queen with her life. Was she doing the opposite of that?

The short time she spent with Methira navigating the peevish forests of Mytherios had only served to rekindle their bond. And her loyalty.

No, she couldn't just fly away and leave the queen to her own fate. She had to turn back and help her queen.

With a groan, she slowed in her skyward ascension.

"What are you doing?" Solana snapped. Josie turned to stare at Spektra. Her face was long and drawn with grief. Which was how the rest of the group looked.

"I am going back to help," Spektra announced. Her huge wings flapped gracefully as she hovered in the yellow sky. "I can't just leave her alone, she'll die."

Solana hissed. "And you think that I do not know that?" she asked, "you seriously believe I am finding it any easier to just fly away from her? She is my queen."

Spektra looked away. She didn't want to meet Solana's eyes. She feared that if she did, then the tears behind her eyes would flow uncontrollably like water from a broken dam.

"Spektra," Solana called in a soothing voice, "I know that you are sworn to protect the queen, but it seems right now that you are doing the opposite…"

"It doesn't seem like—" Spektra interjected "—I am doing the exact opposite!"

"Spektra," Solana called in a grave voice, "right now, the only way we can save the queen is to avenge her. Going back there will kill her and the other fairies that look up to us."

"I don't get it." It was Andy who spoke now. "How can going back there possibly kill her? What's going to kill her is us not turning around to help."

"Andy," Josie said. Her voice was as soft as the clouds around them. When Methira was with them the clouds had looked like beds of soft and yellow cotton. Now, it just lacked any expression at all.

"Andy," she called again, "if we go back, Methira would die in grief. She already blames herself for the fall of the fairies. If she sees us fall into Dromos' hands, then all hope would be lost: for her, for us, and for the fairies."

Andy's eyes closed. And for the first time in a long while, he didn't try to hold back the tears. "She is my friend! She can't die!" he said in a broken voice.

Solana looked away. It would be harder to convince them if they saw her in tears as well. Someone had to be strong for everyone, and that someone would usually wind up being referred to as heartless, even if they did feel the same pain as everyone else.

"We have to leave now," Solana said in a firm voice. "If you return, then you will die alone. The fairies would miss you but won't have the time to mourn you—"

"Solana!" Spektra snarled.

"—because they'd be too busy dying to care, and it'd be your fault," Solana added. Her breath was long and heavy. She continued, "And there is a healthy chance Dromos will not hurt a hair on her head until he's found them."

By them, Solana meant Andy and Josie.

Spektra took a deep breath and closed her eyes. When she opened them again, they were icy and resolute. If there was any regret or emotion at all, then it was buried a hundred miles behind her pupils.

"Let's go, Solana," said Spektra. "You are right. This is the only way. If we build a capable force, then it won't be the usual slaughter, it'd be war."

Andy was not as adept at pretending everything was fine. His eyes were the color of wine pressed from the fruits of pain. He sniffed but uttered no words. What was there to say?

Josie studied her brother. His eyes were red and teary, but she could see that they were also decided. He had managed to make a decision over the time. She hoped it wasn't one she'd come to regret.

Her eyes were drawn to Dromos and his undead army in the not-far-enough distance. From her height, Dromos and his army looked like tiny crumbs of black pepper scattered over a white floor. Tiny crumbs of poisonous bread.

Her eyes had been locked with Dromos for a moment. But that quick glance was enough to remind her of all the memories she worked so hard to forget. Memories like how she had needed to fight Dromos when she went to rescue Andy from his lair.

To be honest, it wasn't a fight at all. It was more like a game of hide and seek. And many times, she thought her life would end, especially if Dromos managed to lay a hand on her. But she had gotten lucky.

And she also managed to get him infuriated. It had been a joy watching him rage helplessly when she had escaped from him. But now she was within his grasp again, and that wasn't even the worst part. She still had to go to his lair.

If he knew that much, he'd probably just be cooling off in his horrible cave, waiting like a hungry lion for its sure prey to come to it. She gave a tired sigh.

Solana turned and burst further ahead, Spektra was behind, following closely.

The tiny speck of breadcrumbs kept getting smaller until there was nothing but a blanket of clouds between them.

Methira watched Spektra and Solana disappear from the corner of her closing eyes. She could be at ease now. Not that there was any point trying to fight. She was immensely outnumbered, but what kept her to the ground was the force from Dromos's magic.

She could neither move a limb nor wing.

"Hello, vanquished queen of the not-so-lively Mytherios," Dromos quipped.

Methira wanted to roll her eyes. He was one to talk, certainly. But she wished she could give him a decent piece of her mind.

"Ratifi," Dromos called.

The old demon creeped forward, the one-hundred-and-one eyes sprinkled over his body rolled about in their positions.

"Command me, my lord," he bowed.

Dromos gave a low growl. "You will take this bug to my lair," he said, "but in the event that you have no use for your head again, you can make the simple mistake of letting her escape."

Ratifi swallowed. Dromos continued.

"I will be swift, and there will be no mercy," he said.

"You have my word, sir," Ratifi replied. He raised his head and snaked towards Methira's limp body, bent over it and scooped her up.

"Take her to my lair," said Dromos. He leered at Methira. "I have a few questions to ask her, and I have no doubt she would confess or be made to."

Ratifi snickered in support of his master.

Dromos turned to Taurus, the dark goblin who had been silent all the while.

"Ratifi will be taking the queen back to the lair, and I will be going there too. You will control this army and find me the girl and the boy. Have I made myself clear?"

"Yes, my lord, Dromos," Taurus replied and gave one of his performer's deep bows. To defy Dromos was to court death, and to disobey him was to seek destruction.

The same portal that had brought Dromos appeared overhead. Ratifi made the first entry with Methira's limp figure in his huge hands.

Dromos gave his army one last sweeping look. It was formidable, this army he raised for himself. It was Invincible. You could wipe out a large army of men, orcs, and even the sleek and haughty elvish race. You'd kill them and they'd die. But what blade could you wield against an army that was already dead? Would you bring steel made by the ancient dwarves or blades carved by elder elves? Could you summon the playful magic of the fairies?

He had expected war when he first arrived. The elder fairies were his aim. It was such a shame he hadn't arrived on time. Or maybe they were fortunate to have gone before his return.

Instead of a worthy foe, he had been met by entertainers. Believers in the abstract notions known as happiness and love.

Love didn't exist. It was subject to conditions. And conditions changed. The only thing that was constant was death, and death was what he brought.

He would sweep misery over the rest of the fairies. He would snuff out their little lights. He would kill their hopes and the hopes of whoever thinks he was going to fail. He was Dromos, lord of the Underworld.

Dromos roared. His undead army trembled at the sound of his voice.

"Yes, fear me and live. "Disobey me and be wiped out of life and death."

Without another word or thought, he turned around and was lifted into the glowing portal above.

As soon as Taurus knew that Dromos was gone, he raised his head. The same went for that Ratifi snake. All that was left was him, bringing glory and power to himself and his people.

"Men of the undead," Taurus called in a loud voice. His hands were thrown behind him as he paced to and fro before Dromos's army.

"The queen of the fairies has been captured," he said, "all that is left before you can be released is for the child Josie, and her brother Andy to be brought before Dromos. Do this and you will find rest."

The entire army groaned and heaved. The march began. And this time even more feverishly than before.

Dead men don't find staying on earth comfortable. It is like staying in a hell within a hell. The dead are meant to stay in the Underworld or the Realm of Light. Any other place is torture worse than the simultaneous bite of a thousand scorpions.

Taurus raised a hand up and pointed forward. The instruction was both unsaid and clear.

The army lunged forward, marching towards their own relief and to the doom of the fairies.

Let Mytherios mourn. Let its forest weep. Let its rivers cease their flow for sorrow. The army of the undead was here, and whatever it touched would become as one of it. Dead.

CHAPTER SEVEN

AFTER TWO DAYS OF FLYING IN MODIFIED ZIGZAGS, and diving into rivers and mud to wash off their scent to shake off the undead army chasing after them like bloodhounds, the white caps of the Moon Mountains appeared before Josie, Andy and the fairies.

The Moon Mountains were said to be magical creatures that had lived very long lives but had now fallen asleep after watching over countless generations. They would never be roused from their dead slumber.

"Follow me," Solana said to Spektra before gliding towards the ravine in the heart of the mountains.

As they made their way deeper into the ravine, the white sheets that covered the mountains began to fade. By and by, the ravine started to grow darker slowly but surely. Eventually, the light blotted out completely. The sun was unable to reach into the depths they now cruised through.

"Where are we going?" asked Josie. There was a slight whimper in her voice.

"Good thing I am not the only one left in the dark," Andy said.

Spektra groaned. "This is no time to play with words, Andy," she cautioned, barely stifling a laugh herself.

"That is especially hard to do if you have been falling for the past one hour," he snapped.

"Relax," Solana said, "we've been down here only eight minutes."

"Oh," Andy exclaimed, "that is comforting."

Even though they couldn't see, the children could feel the air around them get cooler. They could also feel every turn, bend and dive the fairies made. This ravine was not one ravine. It was a network of ravines.

"So, how do you fairies see your way in this pitch blackness?" Andy asked.

"Magic," replied Solana and Spektra at once. They slowed down almost to a halt.

"Are we not th…"

Josie never finished her sentence and for a good reason too.

The words had barely left her mouth when a blinding, bright blue light seemed to have been switched on. Lights appeared to be glued against the rocky walls of the large chamber they were in. Her eyes snapped shut. Josie opened her eyes slowly to get used to the intensity of the light. It was all wrong. Lights?!

Sprinkled along the walls of the large chamber was a mass of specks of blue light, like small stars scattered across a dark sky.

"The fairies…" Andy muttered. He was stunned. And speechless. The fairies still lived, and so many of them at once. It was…

"Unbelievable," Spektra acknowledged.

"Spektra, Andy, Josie – meet the children of Mytherios," announced Solana.

Methira stirred from her unconsciousness back to life. She felt a terrible pang of pain running through her body like a burning river.

Her lips parted to call Andy and Josie. Her mind wondered if she was thinking of current events or things that had happened days or hours ago. She couldn't remember for sure, but the memories slapped her in the face like iron fists.

The last clear thing she remembered was that Dromos's terrible undead army had been advancing at a speed that could be fueled only by the dark magic Dromos wielded. And she had put up a shield to stop them.

Maybe 'stopping' was not the right word. No, stopping them was definitely an exaggeration. She had never intended to stop them. And it was impossible anyway, but she *had* tried to slow them down…at least, long enough for Spektra and Solana to take the kids away to a safe distance. Were they safe? Or had they somehow fallen prey to Dromos's sheer wickedness?

With an effort, she opened her eyes and propped herself up from the hard, jagged rocky floor she had slept on.

"Oh," someone sneered in a voice that was altogether horrible, "the princess is awake."

Methira sat up. Her hands were like strawberry jelly, and her bones felt the same way.

"It is queen, you reptile brain," she mocked.

She somehow managed to rise to her feet. *Oh, this is just nice,* she thought.

It was easy to deduce that she was in Dromos's lair. His crudely hewn-out throne stood visible from the other side of the bar. And yes, she woken up in a cell.

Ratifi stood before her in the cell. His towering height reminded her of the now-extinct race of the Giants.

Speaking of races and extinction, hers was on the very brink of it now. One wrong move, or no move at all — which was in itself a move — and it would all be over, even before it had started.

Methira raised a hand up and slammed it on the floor. Nothing happened. Normally, that was supposed to conjure a portal. She hadn't used it because Dromos had somehow learned how to track the signatures from her magic. What a waste; he had caught her all the same.

Ratifi gave a cruel laugh. "Ha, ha!" he said. "In here, your magic is like the sun trying hard to light up the ocean floors. But no matter how much it burns, it'll never work."

Methira scoffed. Then without a warning, she threw a punch at Ratifi's face and he doubled up.

"Who said I needed magical powers?" said Methira victoriously.

Not even Methira could explain how she went from feeling good for punching Ratifi in the face to feeling like she was being wrapped in the grip of a basilisk. She felt her legs lift off the ground. Her wings had retracted into her body reflexively. Her voice rang out in pain.

"Ah, scream some more."

It was Dromos. Methira tried to bear the pain to deny him the pleasure of seeing her cry or cower before his terrible visage.

But Dromos was prepared for that.

"Cry, you fly," he snarled.

Her eyes snapped shut and her face contorted in severe pain. Veins she never knew existed reared to the surface under the pressure. It felt like she was trapped in a gorge and the walls were closing in against her.

He grunted in satisfaction and released his hold on her.

Methira whimpered as her body hit the hard floor. She could see Dromos in her hazy vision. He occupied the seat which had, up to a few seconds ago, been empty.

"You slept for two days and a couple of hours," Dromos said. His voice was as heavy as the rumbling of thunder. "Not that you had a particularly great sleep. You kept screaming out the names of people that I am very sure are long dead by now."

A frightened chill ran through Methira's veins. She could only hope that she did not give up her people in her sleep.

"But of all the names you mentioned, only two interested me at all," Dromos continued, cutting through her thoughts.

Methira stiffened. Andy and Josie.

Dromos chuckled. "From your response, I am quite convinced that you know those I speak of." He stood from his rocky throne and began to walk towards the cage she was in.

Ratifi had risen to his feet and was beside the door. His face was seething with rage and ire.

"But just so we are absolutely on the same page," he continued (he was just outside her prison now – the bars were all that stood between them), "I speak of the two human children, Andy and Josie."

His eyes met hers.

"Where are they?"

Up till that moment, Methira had never looked into Dromos eyes. And now that she did, she wished she hadn't. The hate she saw there was horrible. But she had seen it, and she couldn't unsee it now.

She gulped.

"I don't know," Methira replied.

Dromos didn't look very satisfied.

Still, he did nothing except to turn around and walk back to his seat.

"Let me warn you," he said without looking back, "you are in my lair, my stronghold, my grip. Anything that does not obey me, everything that refuses to bow to me, anything at all, I will crush it, like an insect trapped in the palm of a hand."

A foreboding. Something assured Methira that Dromos wasn't joking. Her time was limited. He'd crush her just as he promised. Unfailingly.

Andy and Josie were awed by the sight before them. Fairies, all bright and beautiful, in various shades of blue and flickering hues of green. However, one thing was obvious: the dark tint of sorrow and devastation that lined their lights. Each one smiled, but only faintly, almost as though they were forcing a smile.

It was always so. The product of war is a pronounced victory for one side and loss on the other. But even then, both factions are left with gaping losses and breathing pains. How much more a case that wasn't a war but a massacre. To watch one's loved ones die without so much as the chance to fight left a fellow too broken inside. Solana looked at all of them. Her eyes were filled with courage and sympathy.

"I have seen the queen," Solana announced, "Methira is alive."

An excited murmur broke out among the fairies.

"Then where is she?" a young fairy asked.

"On our way here, we were pursued by Dromos's undead forces."

The murmur died away slowly. Their wings and shoulders fell in anguish.

"She stayed behind to save us…and them." Solana pointed to Josie and Andy.

The murmur grew again into an excited chatter.

Spektra cleared her throat. "Methira believes that these children could be the key to our deliverance."

There were cries of "What?", "No way!", "How is that possible?", and "They're just kids, human kids."

"How is that even possible?" one of the fairies asked, "they are young, and they're humans. What could they possibly do to help us?"

The murmur grew loud again. Andy and Josie took a step back and then a couple more. They would probably have run into the blinding darkness if Spektra had not held them comfortingly on the shoulders.

A sudden anger sparked in Spektra. Her body began to glow a fiery red.

"Listen to me sisters," she began. The noise quieted down quickly. It was not every day that a black fairy shone her light.

"The queen, Methira, believed that these children hold the key to our deliverance...."

A loud murmur temporarily interrupted Spektra's train of thought.

"... And maybe she is right, because they have been to the Dromos lair once and they came out unscathed."

Josie wanted to say something against that. She didn't come out physically wounded, but she did have enough fear to last her a lifetime. She did, however, manage not to interrupt Spektra.

"Not one of you has ever gone close to Dromos. If you are alive today, that's why — because you have never neared Dromos, but they have. And they survived it."

The fairies looked at the children with a new admiration now. Meeting Dromos was as fatal as jumping off a cliff without wings. Maybe worse.

Solana saw that Spektra's words had borne fruits and decided to capitalize on it.

"The queen wants to release the four old warriors. And, as you all know, there's a reason Dromos chose that mountain for a lair. It is so we never reach it. No matter how hard we try.

"But things will be different this time, and if it isn't, who cares? Going after Dromos with hopes of a deliverance is infinitely better than sitting here waiting for him to come to us, because I know that he *will* come to us.

He will scourge the earth and turn the universe upside down if that's what it takes to find us.

"But let's spare him the trouble and the effort, and the boredom of everything going just the way he had it all planned. We will pay him a visit in his own home. We will avenge our people and purge our lands free of Dromos. Never again will he rule in this land. Mytherios is ours to prosper in."

An agonizing silence rang across the chambers. For a special moment, the only sound that could be heard in the room was the low hum of the fairy lights.

A fairy stood out from the rest, "I will fight for my queen!"

Another joined her, saying the same thing. And then another, and another, until there were none left who would not lay down their life for their queen.

Solana turned to Spektra. She looked less enthusiastic. Spektra put a hand on her shoulder.

"Don't worry, you made the right choice."

CHAPTER EIGHT

THE WIND AROUND THE FAIRIES' SAFE HAVEN blew not relief, but darkness and tremor over everything that lived within ten leagues of it. And why not?

A little distance away (*little* because the folks in question aren't regular humans, or elves, or horsemen) was the undead army led by Taurus, dark lord of the goblins, stalwart of Lord Dromos. If it were a normal army, the distance would have been two days of hard marching. And no army attacks after two days of such litany of a march. Unless, of course, it was an army that never tires: an army of the dead.

The birds were seen by the fairies' lookouts; they were flying in their droves and multitudes over and past the ravine. It meant one thing: their homes in the forest were being torn apart and they had been forced to migrate out of season. Who wouldn't when their lives were at stake?

Moving towards the same direction, to the setting of the sun, you could see the fistful of black dust gathering like the fiery clouds of a thunderstorm in the distant horizon. They were fast approaching with the charge of a raging bull.

Among the fairies preparing their bows and arrows and other makeshift weapons against a formidable enemy, panic spread like a plague. It was silent yet devastating.

You could see the fear masked by involuntary courage. You could see that very fear shake their fingers, tremble their lips, and send cold shivers down their delicate frames and wings.

Fairies are such great creatures, and this particular race had evolved to bring healing to a torn world, peaceful dreams to a horrible night, and happiness wherever it was they went.

But it wasn't lovely how alone they felt right now. They, who used to put smiles on the faces of others, now lacked any reason at all to have one themselves.

Josie and Andy sat at a round table hewn out of the rocks found in the ravine. It was smooth and soft at the edges. The underground city of the fairies was lit with lights of varying colors. It looked like a bee colony: busy and wary.

A fairy carrying a leaf sack kicked her own foot and fell. Andy and Josie ran to help.

"Are you alright?" asked Andy. He put a hand on the fairy's shoulder. Josie was picking up the small orbs that had fallen out of the leaf bag.

"Should I be truthful or lie and save your ears the lamentations?" she asked.

This fairy wasn't as old as Spektra or Methira, but she wasn't exactly a child. If she was human, 'young adult' would have been her title. Andy swallowed.

"Speak the truth," he said. But he already knew what the truth was. He just did not want to hear it. It was still easy to believe the army of the dead marching aggressively towards them was nothing but an illusion created by playing too many video games and reading all sorts of old scrolls and books.

"I am scared," the fairy said.

Josie walked up to her and joined her on the floor. Andy followed suit. Other fairies carrying one war provision or the other breezed past them on either side.

"Everybody is scared," Josie replied in a quiet whisper.

"Do you think we are all going to die?" the fairy asked. Her eyes were small and as blue as frozen oceans.

"Everybody's going to die," said Andy. "You're going to die, I am going to die, we are all going to die. Just not today. We still have a war to fight."

The fairy craned forward. "Do you really believe we are going to win?"

Andy gave a bittersweet smile. "I think we are going to survive."

The fairy stood up. She still had the fear in her eyes, but it was more obscure now. She curtsied a bow and turned her way.

Andy and Josie rose from the floor.

"I don't know what to expect from this war, Andy," Josie began, "but I have a feeling that things will be different, somehow."

"We will survive this, but I do not know how," Andy said. He tried to think. "To survive at all, we need to beat this deadly force marching with murderous intent towards us. After which, the matter of releasing the ultimate warriors from their golden prisons has to be revisited."

"Andy, Josie, come over here for a quick debriefing." It was Spektra. She stood over the large, round stone table where Andy and Josie had been before the fairy tripped. Aside from Spektra, five other fairies were present at the table, including Solana.

"I will not waste our time on vain ramblings," Spektra began. Her black armor seemed to shine twice as brightly. "We all know which foe is knocking on our doors: dead men dragged from the Underworld. Creatures of magic, *dark* magic. And yet they are not creatures, because that would mean they were created by Dromos. No, instead, they were summoned forcefully from the Underworld."

"They are magical beings. To fight them with steel and blade will yield the same result as cracking a rock open with an egg. We must fight them back with the one element that brought about their existence in the first place… Magic."

The other fairies, save Solana, threw quizzical glances at each other.

Solana rose. She was still as beautiful as ever. "Spektra and I have done some research and planning of our own." She pulled out a spear with what appeared to be a crystal at the tip. "This is a spear, and yet it is not just any spear. The crystal tips are like magical tanks. They will carry their holder's magic and make a weapon of it."

One of the fairies raised a hand. "But we are fairies," she said, "and fairies are not supposed to hurt anyone. Good or bad, living or dead."

There was silence.

Solana sighed. "On the contrary, Evie, we will be doing the army of the dead a big favor by sending them back to where they belong. Humans will suffer terrible pain if they visit the Underworld while still alive. The same goes for these soldiers; they groan in pain, begging to be sent back to the land of the dead."

"And we have a queen to save," Andy added.

"Evie, do you understand Solana's words?" asked Spektra. Evie replied affirmative with a nod of the head.

"We cannot allow them to overwhelm us in the ravine. Even though we have lights to see in the dark, they easily outnumber us, and we should never forget they come from a darkness only death can conjure," Spektra explained.

"Instead," Solana continued, "we will gather at the canyon here, and hold our ground. Our rear and flanks will be protected by the high mountains and terrific terrain. So, they will try to push their way through a single entrance. The frontline will curve in a semicircle to give us the advantage of numbers and we will even be able to outflank them."

"What about Taurus?" asked Josie, "Methira says he is as crafty as any devil that walked the earth."

"That is true," Spektra said, "I plan to keep him busy, personally. The army of the dead is like a mindless tentacle when there is no one to control them. Strong but aimless."

"He will be prepared for that," Andy warned.

"We know," replied Solana. "We are, however, hoping he will not be prepared enough." She gave a shrug. It was their best shot. And really, what other choice did they have?

To win any war, one has to first believe there is a chance of victory, no matter how minute it seems. The first war always happens internally first in the head, and then the heart.

Andy sighed. "You know, I think there is a fat chance we will win this war."

The rest smiled. Too often than not, they had been so immersed in their fear of the enemy approaching that they had completely forgotten the enemy within. The fear that lurked in the eyes of the inexperienced fairies.

A man pees himself at the sight of the enemy. The war is already lost. A graceful fairy trips over her own feet and falls. Did she forget she had wings? Or perhaps, the fear that snuck in through the shadows, like a lion on the prowl, was getting the most of her and many others.

They would overpower the darkness without, only after vanquishing the obscurity within.

Taurus made his new army construct a carriage for him from the woods of Mytherios, and thereafter they bore him on their shoulders. All the dark goblin did was sleep as the mindless army ferried him on their heads and shoulders.

The white mountain loomed from afar.

"Nearly there," he chuckled after waking. "Nearly there."

He fell back on the carriage again, his eyes staring at its wooden roof. If anything, his plan was unfolding into fruition.

The best way to own land is to first drive out its inhabitants or push them to the insatiable brink of extinction. Then, dispose of all weapons of war, even if that meant getting rid of a certain warlord of the dead.

He, himself wasn't a bad sorcerer. He knew it. He had fought Methira ten times and nearly won her twice. She had kicked him in the butt every other time.

He snarled. It was a good thing he never took any of his guards with him whenever he went on such encounters. It was shameful being spanked by a female butterfly.

But that was going to be over soon. This dead army was eager to convert more people to its endless realm.

He chuckled again. Death was probably the only thing in the world that didn't discriminate. It didn't care if you are an elf, a witch, sorcerer, dark goblin or sweet fairy. It'd still gobble thee up, nonetheless.

Not even Dromos was invincible to the icy cold hands of the beauty known as Death.

On the morrow, or at the latest, the day after, the fairies would be reduced to flames, and no phoenix would be born from the resulting ashes.

He laughed again.

The fairies had always prided themselves on peace and order. They believed every single time that they had everything figured out, but they did not.

Life is meant to be unraveled slowly like a flower opening to the morning sun, or to the night bat. But did the fairies ever believe that? No. Instead, they shared candies to all the races and danced and sang and barred themselves from the outer world.

Did Dromos not once crush their seemingly perfect shield like it was a thin slice of ice? And now, they scattered like bees without a colony or a queen. But who knows, perhaps, that was enough to get them to sting again.

He'd find out soon enough if the butterflies still flapped their wings helplessly, hoping the blind enemy would love the art tattooed on it, or maybe, just maybe, they had learnt to sting back when attacked.

CHAPTER NINE

METHIRA'S EYES SLOWLY OPENED AGAIN TO the horrible nightmare she found herself imprisoned in. She'd drifted into a torturous sleep heavy with brackish tears and endless screams, and when she woke, it was to the monstrosity of Dromo's grinning face, or the haughty sneer of his henchman, Ratifi.

A long link of heavy ring-chain was attached to her lips and secured to the rocky floors of her prison. He'd come again soon to taunt her and pressure her into giving up the rest of the fairies. Not that it was up to her to do that, she was yet to see them herself.

Something thudded, then she heard the scratching sound of metal being dragged against the stony floors. No, he was coming again. She braced.

"Well, well, well," he began, "I hope you enjoyed your beauty sleep. It is especially good for people who used to be queens to sleep away their problems. It beats squalor, you see."

He was dragging a large box that was the size and shape of four coffins joined side by side. The box was made of gold. It had markings and drawings in ancient fairy language written on it.

"Tell me, Methira, are your people really coming to open this box here? As far as I am concerned, it is too large for one or even two tiny fairies to airlift. I could, however, help them with that. All you have to do is tell me where to take it and this will be over."

Methira scoffed. Dromos might have sounded like a simple bully, but he wasn't, never had been and never would be. He was a madman obsessed with revenge. And one day, he would realize that revenge doesn't always bring the catharsis we anticipate, so he'd ask for more. Half of the world, and one day, all of it.

"You worry yourself too much, Dromos," Methira managed to say. "I am sure they appreciate your offer and would like to thank you for your generosity. But we will pass on this Trojan horse."

Dromos burst into a cynical laughter. When he wanted to, he could be scary.

"It's not even a horse," he snarled, "It's all of your hope. This is all the weapon your tiny people need to save themselves, all of your hopes, and yet it adorns the palace of the same god you want to unleash them on."

"Yes," Methira said with a weak smile, "we considered logistics and decided it'd be easier to find a place to bury you in your own cave."

"It—it's a palace, not a cave," he warned in a low voice.

Methira knew she should be quiet. That voice meant he was getting pissed off, and she'd be the one to suffer the pain. But she couldn't resist getting a kick out of the dark lord.

"Okay," she began, "it's a cavy palace."

Dromos growled.

Methira felt it happening again. Her legs were losing contact with the ground. Her bones had the feeling of being crushed within her. She screamed.

Dromos laughed. It was what he wanted, always. He loved it. He would always love it. It pleased him to bring pain onto the fairies. And now that they were on the brink of extermination, he'd stretch his hands to other races and other land.

Methira landed on the stone floor. She shook terribly.

"It matters nothing whether you tell me where the rest of your minions are or not. Taurus is on his way to the white mountains as we speak," Dromos said with an air of triumph.

Methira shuddered. That was true.

Fairies are not exactly nomadic. They are social and will always find a place to settle down in their droves as the family that they are. You will never find the fairies where the birds cannot settle.

"They will not be there," Methira spat. But her words were far from convincing as she found it hard to believe them herself. Dromos took no note of this inconsistency. He was victorious either way.

"If they are not there, then we will continue to scour the outlands of Mytherios. Surely, they will be somewhere nearby. Their dependence on magic promptly ensures that they can't be too far from Mytherios. They cannot even afford to leave Mytherios."

The weather was not exactly cold, but Methira shivered and sweated at the same time. How did Dromos get to know so much about them? She gripped the chain with both hands and snarled at him.

"You will pay for this, Dromos. You will pay for every single life you have taken. Every innocent drop of blood you shed on Mytherios's soil will be wrung out of you."

"Indeed," he said in a low mocking voice, "I do not see how that is possible, in this world or the next. And besides," he sat on the golden box holding the four guardians, "just how do you plan to do that?"

She did not know the answer to that. No, she didn't even have the slightest clue how it was going to happen. But in the part of the soul where we are never wrong, the part that helps us hold on to the laughable probabilities that make up our dreams, she felt things would happen differently.

He had been winning for far too long. And life always gave a break to both the victor and the loser. It was the fairies' turn now. She knew it. But it was foolish to argue with him. He would never believe it. And if he did, it would only make him more cautious, more sneaky, and ultimately harder to beat.

"Well," she said, "I don't know yet."

Dromos laughed like a lunatic.

"Of course, you don't, because there is no way at all."

He burst into laughter again. A bellow that sent shrill into the heart of those that heard it.

But Methira did not dread it this time. She did not envy it at all. Her time would come, and when it did, she'd teach him how to laugh.

"The dead army!" a male fairy screamed as he ran inside. Spektra and Solana had ensured that a proper watch was set at all hours of the day. That way, they'd be able to monitor the ever-aggressive march heading towards them.

"Your training, fairy!" Spektra snapped. In her head, she wondered if snapping at him would draw him out of his panic or if it would push him past the borders of hysteria.

"The dead army is two leagues out and fast approaching," the fairy said in a calmer voice, "They'd be upon us in four hours."

Spektra glanced at Solana. Their eyes met.

"It's time," Solana said firmly.

Spektra nodded in affirmative. "It is."

"My brothers and sisters," Solana said. She turned to face the various eyes staring at her.

The eyes are indeed the window of the soul. You stare at them and see more than two circles enclosed within each other. Through the eyes, you can see a man's fear, his joy, his pain and his anger, and all you have to do is look through it, not at it.

The eyes that stared at Spektra and Solana were owned by magical creatures. But everything that had a soul sought for the same thing in varying ways. A dog's eye would portray the same fear as frightened child's eye would.

Solana felt her breath drag in her lungs. Her weight shifted from one leg to the other. She did not know what to say for sure. The queen had a voice that was just as stentorian as soothing. It was she who always knew what to say.

"We have come a long way since we were sacked from our place in the heart of Mytherios, our home. Never did we think that the day would come when we'd fall like lambs off the cliff of survival. But that is exactly what happened. We have lost fathers, mothers, friends, loved ones, siblings, even our usual life.

"I don't know if we'd defeat that lifeless army out there. What I do know is that I am so tired of running and hiding and being hunted. I am tired of being grieved all day long. I know fairies are here to give life. But the army out there has none of that. Instead, it has taken the forest with it.

"Do you see how barren the forests are? How evil and darkness lord over the daytime. Let's not talk about the nights. I will take Mytherios back. I will save my queen from Dromos's filthy hands, and if he is so unlucky to have hurt her in any way, I'll make him wish he never existed. Are you with me?"

"Yes, Solana!" chorused the fairies with pride and flying spirits.

"Are you with me?!"

"Yes, Solana!"

"Army of light, take battle positions!"

"I've never seen you like that," Josie said to Solana who blushed painfully. Blushing when there is a war outside your front door is a humanly thing to do.

"She used to teach kids how to sing the flowers to sleep at night. The next song she will be singing will be one of war cries," said Spektra.

Josie and Andy held a spear in their hands.

"You have magic. Make sure you recharge your weapons," Solana told them.

Andy waved dismissively. "Who said anything about us recharging? Today, we will be attacking like wolves."

Solana was intrigued. "And how do these *wolves* attack?"

"In group," Josie offered. "When the magic in the crystal is depleted, we'll swap it with a fairy and continue the fight."

"That's slow, but creative, nonetheless. You should, however, keep to the backline, that way—"

"Not another word from you, Spektra," said Andy. His face was reddened with indignation. "We will fight. Every creature capable of wielding a weapon should fight. Don't you guys have monkeys? Or apes? We could use them now."

"We don't have any of that, Andy," Solana said, "but we hope that you keep safe. Both of you."

But Andy wasn't ready to give in to safety protocols. "We are at war. This is the worst time for safety concerns."

Solana and Spektra closed their eyes in frustration. Josie urged Andy out of the underground hideout.

"It's a peculiarity of his, sorry."

If Taurus did not see the wings flapping busily behind each member of the army before him, he'd have concluded that the elves had left their realm and were here in defence of the fairies.

They were arranged in such fascinating order that he grew irritated with his own army that kept growling and snarling like depraved beasts.

An army of goblins would have at least turned around at this resolute sight. That is, if their legs did not turn to jelly on the spot. There is nothing a goblin hates more than a confident foe.

But this wasn't his army, and he could afford to lose as much as possible.

Speaking of which, what could the fairies possibly do? Taurus got down from his carriage and gave an indolent stretch. Being carried all day long was tough work.

He stared at the terrain again. The fairies looked, if anything, trapped between those mountains. They were walled in by towering white heights. All he had to do was charge right at them. The mouth of the valley looked narrow, but it was okay. He had men to spare.

The fairies would be vanquished line after line, until the earth was colored with their blood. And he'd have a good drink himself.

They numbered a couple of thousand. He had an army of ten thousand. The odds weren't fair, but what could a goblin do other than take what he was offered.

He turned to face his army. Not that they needed any rousing; the urge to return to the Underworld filled them with that much.

His rheumy eyes ran over them again. Mindless and dangerous; this was a certain victory. They'd tear through the fairies like an iron-tipped arrow through the flesh.

"Prepare for battle!" he screamed.

Solana and Spektra clutched their weapons. They had a plan: absorb the attack like an elastic surface, and take out the enemy, or at least as much of him as they could do. Taurus, the slippery goblin, would be kept busy enough.

Today, it was fire on fire. Their survival depended largely on the outcome of this victory. Dromos would not be able to easily summon as many dead again for quite a while, which gave them the chance of a simple 'snatch and grab', with the exclusion of *simple* because it wasn't, and they used the term *grab* because it means the same thing as *snatch*.

But they were nowhere close to that bridge yet. There was no point trying to cross it now.

"For Methira!" Andy yelled.

"For Methira!" the army repeated in a loud chorus.

"For Mytherios!" Josie cried.

"For Mytherios!"

At that moment, they felt twice as large and three times as many.

Let the war… begin.

CHAPTER TEN

THE EVENING SUN BURNED RED OF THICK SOUP and blood. The sky was the color of angry clouds darkened by thunderstorms. There was no breeze, just the wind carrying the sounds of the grave tidings of war from the ghostly embrace of the White Mountains to the ends of Mytherios.

On one side of the war, the winged bodies of fairies, disfigured by death and their manner of passage, carpeted the floor. Their blood inked deathly notes in the book of history, and on the floors of the battlefield, it spread like spilled paint.

On the other side of the war, the undead vanished like the Romans built in one day. The undead leave no bodies behind. Instead, a circle of greenish soot is formed wherever they fall, just as they disappear into the airless wind to never return again.

"Ratifi joined him!" Solana cried to Spektra.

Spektra strained. A dead general was trying hard to make her just like him.

One thing about the battlefield is that it doesn't give you the chance to share a joke you just remembered with a friend, or even information as vital as the fact that your enemies have doubled, and the odds of winning have been effectively halved by that.

"I can't leave here!" Spektra shouted back at Solana just as a blast escaped her crystal spear. Her opponents disappeared and two more took his place, looking like the head of a hydra.

One more thing about the battlefield is this: it never gives you time to think or use your head. You have to create that time. No house is built around the door. In the end, the door is always added after the house is built.

But Solana tried to think. She had to. Ratifi was a formidable enemy. She had seen him ravage her kingdom the first time, even though he did it with help from his mad master. But he was still strong all the same.

Now, if unskilled fairies were to keep attacking him, it'd be disastrous. She felt someone back up against her.

"Andy!"

He turned. There was an unconcerned expression on his face. "You look super excited to see me."

Solana laughed and threw a magic blast at an incoming attacker.

"Oh, well…"

Andy jumped back and threw a magic blast at a phantom behind him. He returned with his shoulders high.

"You were saying?"

Solana rolled her eyes. "Spektra is too busy with the dead generals. She can't find her way out of that flank. I need you and Josie to take on Taurus while I go for Ratifi. We can't let any other fairy face that monster."

Andy narrowed his eyes. "Is that all?" he asked.

Solana tightened her grip around her spear to keep from laughing in the middle of the battlefield. But something told her Andy would, if he wanted to.

"That will be all," she replied and returned to fighting. "I can't believe that boy brought his ego to the battlefield," she muttered to herself as he left.

"What are you doing here, you bilious demon?!" Taurus asked. There was anger written all over his face. He had plans to make this battle *his* victory, his lone effort. And it was going fine until the giant reptile had popped out of nowhere. Well, maybe it wasn't.

"I'm playing hopscotch with the fairies. Want to join?" Ratifi threw back coldly, "Listen, you blistering fool, you'd be totally swept off your feet if I wasn't here. Imagine butterflies stinging like wasps! And it's all Dromos's fault. A creature like you belongs in the pigsty as pig food."

Taurus swallowed. Ratifi was wrong about every single thing he said except the 'butterflies stinging like wasps' part.

The battle had started four hours ago. He thought it strange that the fairies did not move an inch when he attacked. But when his army neared them, the fairies' frontline suddenly depressed, giving them numerical advantage at the front. Especially as it was impossible to out flank them.

Until Ratifi arrived, it had been impossible to break through the fairies' frontline.

"I had everything under control, you idiot!" Taurus threw back.

Ratifi guffawed just as he slapped a fairy out of his way. "Sounds like your self-assessment has shown you how dimwitted you are. Wait till this is over, Dromos will hear of your overwhelming incompetence."

Taurus bit his lower lip.

"Ah! There you are, ugly goblin," Andy announced as he came face to face with Taurus. Josie was going to be right behind him, or so he hoped. He had told her hurriedly, and he wasn't even sure she had heard him at all.

Taurus turned around to face his old adversary. "What is this? Prepared to lose again boy! Do you know how many grown men and fearsome warriors that I have trampled over?"

Andy frowned. "I have no time for fictional statistics. Come over here, and I'll show you not to attack fairies anymore."

Taurus guffawed. "Oh, this is going to hurt."

Andy leered at him. "You have no idea."

Ratifi felt a blast hit him just as he was about to strike his fiftieth fairy of the day. He muttered a curse and turned to face the source. His excessive brows raised apprehensively.

"Methira?" he said.

Solana boiled. "You have no right to say that name, you filthy filth." She made a run for him and struck him at the knees. He fell.

She returned again and hit him at the temples, sending images of stars and celestial bodies floating in his vision.

Ratifi was Dromos's strongest warrior, but he was just as slow as he was large. And Solana was one of the fairies' finest leaders: swift and capable.

He staggered to his feet, shook his head to clear the floating images and snarled.

"You will regret this."

"I already regret not doing more," Solana replied and charged at Ratifi again. She was working just fine.

Solana risked a glance at Andy and saw him taking on Taurus on his own. She should have known. His ego was large enough to be shared among hundreds of people.

With the leaders of the army of the dead distracted, the army weakened considerably, and fairies began to have the upper hand.

An observer viewing from the sky with a hawk's eye would see the flashes of blue thundering out of the crystals wielded by the fairies flashing across the battlefield. Dust rose in thick clouds as the red sun refused to sink into the horizon, almost like it was being held up by some powerful hand.

Maybe it is true that good things don't last forever. At least that's what Andy thought before Dromos showed up, sending a huge shockwave that blasted everyone to the floor. Including his own monstrous creatures.

The state of things exactly one minute before Dromos showed up was this: Taurus was getting the beating of his life from a human who was neither a grown up nor a fearsome warrior, and running away was beginning to look like a splendid idea. Ratifi was wondering why nobody ever told him a fairy could be so fast and dangerous at the same time, and Solana wasn't giving him the time to think too much about it. The fairies were stinging like wasps, bees and scorpions merged into one. Their fears seemed to be taking a nap.

Well, that was how things were before Dromos showed up. Now what happened when Dromos showed up?

A spherical portal opened in the sky above the fighting warriors and Dromos dropped out of it. He landed on his feet and proceeded to slam a great fist into the earth. The wave got everyone sitting looking around in confusion. The wave was so powerful that it could be felt for thousands of miles.

Methira was slung over his shoulder. She didn't seem to be in control of her body. Her strength had failed her completely.

Dromos had a grand scheme. He had brought Methira to the battlefield deliberately. It was a logic that had never failed to work. He lifted her by the hands so all those present could see her. Strike the shepherd, and the flock would scatter into the hands of their predators. Their spirits would be broken.

It worked. A ghostly silence ruled the battlefield when the fairies sighted their beloved leader hanging limply from their greatest adversary's grip.

Meanwhile, Taurus and Ratifi did the best they could — which was terrible by the way — to not limp as they ran to flank Dromos on either side.

They didn't say it, but every part of them was screaming, thank you Lord Dromos for saving me from eternal suffering.

Dromos hissed at the sight of his limping commanders. He returned his gaze, well, more of a glare, at the fairy army.

"Is this not your queen?" he said in a mocking voice. "Methira, the fairest of fairies in all the lands…"

A fairy sniffed. What do we know about fairies? They are sentimental. This generation are happiness givers, they don't inflict pain, and they don't know how to handle it.

"…See how she hangs, half dead, and fully helpless in my hold."

Methira stirred. She tried to smile but ended up coughing. That didn't help matters, and one of the fairies broke into a loud wail. Another knocked him out.

"So," he opened his fist and let Methira crumble to the floor, "I am going to relieve Mytherios of her pathetic existence, and yours soon enough."

Josie appeared beside Andy. "He is going to kill her," she said.

"I know," Andy said between clenched teeth.

"Well, what do we do? Are we going to just stand here?"

Dromos was looming over Methira now.

"Let's attack him—"

"With what? Last time I hit him with my power it didn't even scratch him!"

Andy glanced at his sister. "Josie, what else do we have? The crystal spears."

"I'm not sure it's going to do much."

Andy didn't think it was going to do much either. To be specific, he didn't think it was going to do anything to

Dromos at all, but they couldn't do nothing. Andy grabbed a crystal spear and handed another to Josie.

"One… Two… Go!"

Together, the siblings surged out of the fairies' ranks and threw huge blasts of energy at Dromos. It was the largest of the battle. Ratifi and Taurus gasped. Solana shuddered. Spektra froze. The rest of the fairies simply bulged their eyes.

Dromos was covered in smoke, and for a moment, no one could see him at all. Just a cloud of smoke plumed around him.

"Do you think we got him?" Josie asked Andy.

"Of course not!" replied Dromos. He was totally unharmed. "The two of you will be coming with me as well. We have a lot to talk about. But first," he returned to Methira who was still lying on the floor, "let's end this one."

He walked up to her and lifted one huge leg. It is best to not say what he planned to do, but whatever it was, it would have left Methira irredeemable.

But the war wasn't over, and it had no plans of ending just yet.

A loud noise, like the howl of a stormy wind, tore through the battle ground.

Dromos glanced up. There was confusion written all over his face which led the rest to wonder what else was happening.

Suddenly, a white flash tore from the sky and struck the Dromos camp. The army of the dead reacted violently to this. They shook terribly and began to crumble like powdery statues.

Dromos glanced around at his army falling to ashes before his eyes. "This is impossible," his thick lips quivered. "What is happening?"

One after the other, his host of dead soldiers fell to the earth like a pile of ash until there was none of them left again. He glanced around him just as the last soldier vanished. A terrible roar escaped his lungs, and his breath came out forcibly.

"Show yourself, you intruder!" he bellowed.

"Here I am," a mysterious voice said in what sounded like a whisper.

Dromos turned around to face his nemesis.

CHAPTER ELEVEN

THE SOURCE OF THE VOICE WAS A FIGURE IN A LONG purple cape that stopped short of reaching the ground as it hovered above it. A long, slender hand from within the cape held a staff that had a glowing crystal twigged over it. The air around this new visitor was quiet.

Taurus shivered. He couldn't shake off the thought that he had joined the wrong ship and his end was now approaching. Mages weren't too hard to recognize.

Methira had managed to muster some strength. The drama unfolding had shifted Dromos' threatening leg and focus away from her. She muttered something and teleported away from where she was, landing besides Josie and Andy.

Solana ran over to her. "Methira, are you alright?"

Spektra joined the small group.

"We don't have time for a reunion. We have to go to Dromos's lair and release the guardians," Methira said. The hope that things might not be entirely over filled her with a new kind of strength.

"Who is that?" asked Andy. He gestured towards the new element in their not-too-sweet party.

Methira's eyes narrowed. She had a suspicion, but whoever it was did not matter right now. What did matter was the fact that they now had a window of time to turn things around in their favor, and that was what she was going to do.

"Come closer, all of you," Methira ordered. They hurdled towards her like newly hatched chicks.

A sizzling sound was heard, and they were gone.

Dromos heard the sizzle and looked away from the apparition. He glanced at Methira's body on the floor, or where it was supposed to be. The floor was there alright, but Methira had gone.

He frowned. He was about to dismiss the thought when another occurred to him. The sizzling sound he heard was definitely Methira disappearing. His eyes lit up in euphoria. She was heading for the guardians.

"Ratifi! Taurus!" Dromos barked. "Come, take care of this insolent guest here."

Taurus blinked. "Why? I think you should do it yourself. As a summoner of the dead to another summoner of the dead."

Dromos hissed. "You incompetent cretin!"

Taurus swallowed. "Uhm, Ratifi? Maybe you should go ahead. I want to give you a chance to show Lord Dromos here your potentials."

Ratifi growled. "You coward! We are attacking at once."

They took a step forward, but that was all they did. The mage raised the staff and tapped the earth with it. A wave of wind, similar to the one Dromos had conjured but twice as strong, lifted Taurus and Ratifi off the ground and sent them crashing against the canyon walls.

Dromos was red hot with anger. He'd destroy this mage and the fairy army at once. But, just as he stepped forward, a great ball of mist engulfed the mage and the fairy army. By the time the mist cleared, they were gone.

He let out a great roar. This was not going according to plan at all. His mind drifted back to Methira who was probably trying to release the guardians. It was a good thing he'd taken the precaution of stowing the box away. That would buy him some precious minutes.

Enraged and unsatiated, Dromos summoned a portal to his lair and stepped into it.

"I think I broke a rib or two," Ratifi said with a groan as he lifted himself off the ground.

"That's good news," Taurus remarked, "I can't think of a part of me that isn't broken."

Methira, Spektra, Solana, Josie and Andy found themselves in one of the many tunnels in Dromos's lair. It was dark, damp and cold.

"Where is this?" Andy asked.

"Dromos's hideout," Methira answered.

There was light at the end of the tunnel.

"Okay," said Andy, "so, what are we doing at Dromos's hideout?" A shudder ran through him as memories of his captivity here haunted his thoughts.

"To find the four guardians," Spektra replied hastily. "Let's make for that light."

"Are we sure it is here?" Andy asked again. Josie searched for his hand in the darkness. She understood him. It wasn't really hard to understand Andy. All that was necessary was to spend a couple of days in the palace of a psychopath.

"Yes," Methira answered, "it is here. He showed it to me."

The rest gasped.

"And why would he do that?" Solana asked, hurrying to walk right beside Methira.

"Because he wanted to taunt me to the best of his abilities and…and make me feel powerless," Methira replied.

"So, did he succeed?" asked Spektra, "At making you feel powerless, did he succeed?"

Methira answered. "I—"

Andy butted in. "When you stand before a fellow like Dromos, lord of the Underworld, the only feeling you can ever muster is helplessness. When he stands before you, it chokes you around the neck, and when he speaks, his voice drains you of your energy. He is like that, is Dromos. And I can assure you, even with our number, the best we can do is pretend we are not helpless."

Spektra gulped. She was a warrior, and she had almost believed that the queen was a weakling for succumbing to Dromos taunts and antics, but hearing now that their numbers didn't offer them any significant advantage left a different flavor in her mouth.

What if they came face to face with Dromos? Would they be able to stop him, or at least survive long enough to release the four guardians?

She knew that Dromos was probably on his way, but a part of her hoped that he was dead, that the mage who suddenly showed up from nowhere had done them a good turn. But good things were hard to wish for these days. It was almost hard enough to wish that they would live long enough to see the next moment. How much harder could it be to wish seeing the death of the infamous lord of the Underworld?

The company found themselves in a large chamber. The chamber had several tunnels leading to it. There was a large lantern burning from a stick on the wall. The yellow light from the lantern flicked and moved causing the shadows on the rough walls to dance like puppets.

The air was dry and dusty here.

"I will be happy when all this comes to an end," Andy said. A tired sigh escaped his lips.

"I wish this was all a bad dream," Josie added.

"No way. We have put in too much effort and gone through too much pain for everything to turn out to be some severe form of hallucination. We will conquer here, and dream of our victory."

Methira didn't know what to say to that. She wished it was just a dream, like Josie had said. She sincerely wished it was just her worst fears gathering like an evil army in her sleep. That each event had been nothing but a sweat in her sleep.

That is what she hoped for too.

She didn't care whatever pain she had felt. If all of that pain would be reversed, all those lives restored, and Mytherios became the cynosure of beauty again, even at the cost of her sanity, she'd give it a go.

But it wasn't a dream, and the sooner she realized it, the better.

"Honestly," began Solana, "I didn't know we'd make it this far," she said. "It just looks so bleak, that nothing we do seems to matter at all. And suddenly, there's this unbelievable chance we'd bring an end to it."

Methira nodded. "I know, Solana. I know." She held Solana's scarred hands and gave them a gentle squeeze. "It will be alright Solana, I promise. You and I will see Mytherios rise to give hope and joy again."

Andy turned to Josie and whispered, "I wish Methira wouldn't make such promises."

Josie winced. "Why, Andy?"

"Because a promise like that is not for her to keep."

"Oh, let her be, Andy. Let her be."

Dromos walked into his lair through the portal. He sniffed; they were there. His eyes darted around furtively. He was about to go into one of the tunnels but stopped in his tracks.

He clenched his fist and gave a sharp hiss. His grotesque throne stared at him in the face. Yes, he'd wait here, and let them come to him.

And when they did, sparing them wouldn't even be a valid word. He'd kill them till they were beyond death. It'd be worse for the human siblings. He only wanted to chain them in a nice cage he'd prepared before, but that offer was no longer available. No, he'd show them differently now.

Dromos settled on his throne, waiting like a lion for its meal. Waiting like Death for its next victim.

Solana felt a cold shiver within her. Something was wrong.

Slowly, she walked away from the rest of the group who were hurdled over, discussing what they knew about the tunnels and the best way to find it.

Solana stepped out of the room just as Andy was mentioning something about wolves and packs. That boy and his wild ideas. Solana thought it would be pleasant to see him infecting the male fairies with his ideas.

She made out of the chamber through a corridor, taking each step with caution and stealth. She bent slightly as she moved forward. Her ears were keen, looking to hear the faintest of noise.

She soon found an entrance to another room. She walked through it. This room was more decorated, but it was rough all the same. The walls were lined with rare animal skulls and horns, and full skeletons ripped out of their owners' bodies.

"I hope that you like my collection," he said.

Solana didn't turn around like she was scared. For the next few seconds, she simply contented herself with the revolting antiques on the wall.

"They are a true representation of your person," she said, and then turned around, "and everything that you stand for, Dromos."

He guffawed with the laughter of a predator stalking a cornered prey.

"And what is my person about, butterfly?"

"Death. Destruction. Desolation."

He rubbed his chin and pressed his knuckles. "So be it."

"Andy and Solana will take that tunnel and see where it leads to," Methira said.

"Okay," Andy replied.

"Solana?" Methira called. Her eyes were still fixed on the drawing she scrawled on the floor. Her head jerked up. "Sola—where is Solana?"

The group murmured words like "I could have sworn she was right here" and "wherever did she go?" and other questions that none of them had answers to.

Methira closed her eyes and tried to find Solana with her magic.

"Oh no," she said just as her eyes flew open. "Solana!" She took off in the same tunnel Solana had passed a little while back.

"Do you really think that you stand the slightest chance against me?" asked Dromos. He and Solana circled each other, like wrestlers in a ring.

"Does it matter what I think?" asked Solana. Her voice faltered a little. Of course, she stood no chance against him. Not even Methira had won against Dromos.

But she'd rather die a thousand times and more than give Dromos the satisfaction of watching her beg for mercy. Maybe Andy had rubbed some of his ego on her.

"Fine," Dromos said in a bland voice, "come to your master."

Solana frowned and ran at him. She lurched into the air and threw a blast at him.

The rest would have at least noticed her absence and were probably on their way right now. All she had to do was drag the fight out a bit.

But Dromos had plans of his own. He flicked away the blast like it was an annoying fly and caught Solana by the neck.

"Death. Destruction. Desolation."

The last sound Solana heard before she died was the snapping sound her neck made as Dromos turned it.

Looks like I wouldn't be seeing the new Mytherios after all, she thought as life slipped away from her.

Methira entered at about the same time that Solana's body fell to the floor. She saw Dromos standing over her, an evil grin stretched across his face.

"Solana!" she screamed.

ABOUT THE AUTHOR

127

James Keith is a knowledgeable professional with almost 20 years of proficiency in the healthcare industry. James has always been an activist for mental health due to his own experiences in the field.
James wants people to be aware of how to deal with emotional, psychological, and social well-being issues and how to stop them from affecting their lives.

Follow James at www.JamesKeith.co.uk